JENNIFER GREENE
Lady of the Island

Silhouette Desire

Published by Silhouette Books New York

America's Publisher of Contemporary Romance

SILHOUETTE BOOKS
300 East 42nd St., New York, N.Y. 10017

Copyright © 1988 by Jennifer Greene

ISBN: 0-373-05463-7

First Silhouette Books printing December 1988

Printed in the U.S.A.

Books by Jennifer Greene

Silhouette Desire

Body and Soul #263
Foolish Pleasure #293
Madam's Room #326
Dear Reader #350
Minx #366
Lady Be Good #385
Love Potion #421
The Castle Keep #439
Lady of the Island #463

Silhouette Intimate Moments

Secrets #221

JENNIFER GREENE

lives on a centennial farm near Lake Michigan with her husband and two children. Before writing full-time, she worked as a personnel manager, counselor and teacher. Mid-1988 marked the publication of her twenty-fifth romance. She claims the critical ingredient to success is a compassionate, kind, patient, understanding husband—who can cook.

Her writing has won national awards from Romance Writers of America, *Romantic Times* and *Affaire de Coeur*. She has also written under the pen name of Jeanne Grant.

This Man Is Dangerous.

His lips were cool and smooth, and pressed against hers with absorbing pressure. She had the quicksilver sensation that he was absorbing her, taking her in, draining her of will and sense.

She told herself to move. She reminded herself that a relationship with any man was out of the question. Any intimate, personal needs she had as a woman had been banished months ago.

And Jarl kissed like danger, smelled like danger, tasted like danger. Not the danger that he would harm her. The terror was that he wouldn't.

A hoarse, half-wild sound broke the silence. It must have come from her, because she heard him murmur something gruff and low and approving. He gathered her up, and the last of her good sense shattered....

Dear Reader:

Happy Holidays to all of you!

This December brings not only three sensational books by familiar favorites—Jennifer Greene, Annette Broadrick and Sara Chance—but wonderful stories from a couple of newcomers: Jackie Merritt and Terry Lawrence. There's also a fabulous Christmas bonus, *'Tis the Season* by Noreen Brownlie, a novel full of the Christmas spirit about the best gift of all—the gift of love.

January marks the beginning of a very special new year, a twelve-month extravaganza with Silhouette Desire. We've declared 1989 the Year of the Man, and we're spotlighting one book each month as a tribute to the Silhouette Desire hero—our Man of the Month!

Created by your favorite authors, you'll find these men utterly irresistible. You'll be swept away by Diana Palmer's Mr. Janaury, (whom some might remember from a brief appearance in *Fit for a King*), and Joan Hohl's Mr. February is every woman's idea of the perfect Valentine....

Don't let these men get away!

Yours,

Isabel Swift
Senior Editor & Editorial Coordinator

One

Jarl popped the lid on his beer, shifted his shoulders until they found a comfortable spot in the chaise longue and put on his sunglasses.

Laziness was a neglected art form. He was fussy on the subject. The Detroit Tigers cap—from the year they'd won the pennant—was essential to a good lazy mood. So were fifteen-year-old cutoffs, bare feet and adjusting one's body to get a precise, perfect angle of the sun.

He tipped his cap to shade his eyes, lifted the beer to his lips and surveyed the king's domain in front of him. The fifteen acres surrounding the petal-shaped cove were his. Most Michigan inland lakes were heavily populated by summer vacationers, but not Clover.

Jarl could taste the privacy, and he could smell the clipped grass and deep green woods behind his cottage. Water lip-lapped at the shore like a sleepy man's surf, and the sun was hot—July hot. A few white frosting clouds danced across the sky. The water was a clear, clean blue and cold enough for trout potential.

Diverting his attention—as it always did—was the egg-shaped island in the middle of the lake. His curiosity about the deserted island had mildly nagged at him since he'd bought his property. He could see that its shores were a weed-tangled mess of scrub trees and sumac. He could glimpse a rooftop of a fairly large building on the east end. A falling-down peach orchard dominated the west side. Max, at the bait shop, had told him once that the property used to be a Boy Scout camp years before and also that the property wasn't for sale.

Someone had to own it, but Jarl had never seen anyone on or near it. He debated whether he could swim the dis-tance—it couldn't be more than a mile—but the lake was chopped-ice cold and posed cramp potential for even an experienced swimmer. He could row across to explore, of course, but that involved no challenge at all.

Challenges, however, were not supposed to be on his mind. Laziness was. Chugalugging the last of the beer, he closed his eyes, aware that he was bored out of his mind. Other people did this on vacation all the time, didn't they? Sat. Did nothing. Enjoyed solitude and peace and inactiv-ity without a qualm of workaholic-flavored guilt.

A bee buzzed by. He had a short staring contest with the fat yellow jacket, which then deserted him for the wild pan-sies at the edge of the woods.

Seven more minutes ticked by, then eight. He'd nearly managed an hour of sitting still when he heard a bird's panicked cry. She cried a second time. Mildly swearing at the interruption—token swearing, as he'd have paid a fly for an excuse to move—he lurched out of the lounger. Again he heard the bird's mournful, desperate cry, but it took him a moment to spot the peek of velvet gray in the choked green bush.

The bird was full grown, healthy and plump, but her claws were hopelessly tangled in a mound of fishing wire. When his giant shadow covered her, she made frantic moves to escape. Her cries turned piercing when he gently wrapped a big hand around her wings and scooped her up. From the licensed tag cuffed to her leg, he figured she was a homing pigeon.

"Sssh, sssh," he scolded. She was shaking so violently that he couldn't unwrap the wire. As far as he could tell, she wasn't hurt, just panicked. Her terrified cries jangled the peace of a still afternoon. "Haven't you got an instinct in your head? I'd be the last one to hurt you. You'll be free in a minute. Easy, easy now..."

Freeing her took a lot of stroking, a lot of talk, and ultimately finding clippers in the cottage. She didn't like the clippers, but she didn't try to nip him, which made it obvious that she'd been handled by people before.

Jarl released her on the ground near the lakeshore and backed off, watching to see what she'd do. Mostly she ignored him, which made him crack a smile. Hey, I just saved your life, you turkey, he thought. She fluttered her wings, strutted like a vain woman with a DAR heritage, pecked a little sand and then took off.

Shielding his eyes from the sun, he watched her soar. Curiosity quickened when he realized her flight was beeline straight for his mystery island. In principle the deserted island was an ideal wild bird sanctuary, but the pigeon hadn't been wild. Granted, Jarl was no expert on the subject, but wouldn't a homer logically be headed for home?

Long after the bird disappeared, he couldn't take his eyes off the island. Nothing looked new, nothing appeared different. He could see green leaves tipped silver in the summer wind, the tip of a roof baking under the hot sun, the gnarled old peach trees drooping under the weight of their crop. But no sign of any kind of life.

Discovering where the bird called home was hardly the most monumental problem he'd ever come across. Still, it nagged at him. Little things had a habit of nagging at Jarl. The next morning he loaded his boat with a tackle box, reel and a thermos of coffee. That early, the dew was still heavy and the sky a pastel haze blanketing the smooth lake. His oars barely rippled the water. It was trout-catching time of day, which was his second priority on the morning's agenda.

If he remembered correctly, there was a broken-down dock on the far side of the island. His memory hadn't failed him. The dock was still there, still broken-down, but the spot was still the likeliest place to moor a boat. His oars dug into the sand bottom five feet from shore. Using an oar like a pole, he scuttled the boat closer and jumped out.

Ice water claimed his jeans to midcalf and his bare feet sucked in sand. He ducked his head to grab the mooring rope, and when he looked up again he suddenly saw a child standing in the brush. The little one was three? Four? Anyway, he was tiny, with a shag of thick caramel-brown bangs and huge blue eyes.

"Hi," Jarl said, offering an opening.

The child stood mute and solemn. A T-shirt proclaimed that the boy was a Blue Whale fan. His jeans were battered and a fleck of toothpaste had dried on his cheek. He was thin, built skinny as a whisper, and those big soft eyes took up his whole face. Jarl smiled.

"You live here on the island, or just camping out with your parents?" No response. Jarl nodded. "You shouldn't talk to strangers, should you? I'm thirty-three and I still don't volunteer much to people I don't know. Is your mom and dad around? You don't have to talk. You can just kind of motion where I could find them."

The tyke was more inclined to raise a battered, rusted Fisher-Price bulldozer and hug it tightly to his chest.

"Nice," Jarl commented gravely. "Looks to me like that dozer's done a lot of serious work."

No nod. No grin—just a death grip on the metal-edged bulldozer. Jarl groped for something to say that would put the little one at ease. "I guess I'm trespassing. Curiosity is a chronic fault of mine. You see, yesterday I found a bird in trouble...." At last, a glint of life in those luminous blue eyes. "She flew over to the island here. It wouldn't be your bird by chance? You don't have to talk. You could just nod or shake your head. I just wanted to know if she was okay."

The little boy nodded vigorously, but when Jarl waded a step forward he tensed like a statue. Not a little tense, but nightmare-tense, and the child's eyes turned sapphire-bright with fear. Perplexed, Jarl stood still and said gently, "I won't come any closer, all right? There's nothing to be afraid of. I only wanted to ask you about your bird, and now I'll—"

"Kip!"

The child disappeared faster than a half-wild woods critter. Still startled by the boy's reaction to him, Jarl squinted hard at where the little one had crashed through the brush, then turned toward the sound of the feminine voice.

A woman was striding toward him through the scratchy overgrowth of sumac near the west shore. He noticed *her* second. When a shotgun muzzle was aimed directly for a man's face, he didn't initially much care who was holding it.

"This is private property, mister. Clear out."

She stopped dead four feet from him, close enough that he could see that the two slim feminine hands bracing the gun barrel were shaking violently. His heart started thumping. Copper coated his tongue. Her unfamiliarity with the firearm was obvious but hardly reassuring. People unfamiliar with guns were always the most dangerous.

Turtle slow, his gaze shifted from the gun to the woman's eyes. His peripheral vision absorbed the unessential details. She was barefoot, wearing jeans and a haphazardly-buttoned red shirt. Her hair was a cropped tumble of spiked bangs and gamine curls, a cross between chicory and caramel in color, and similar to the boy's. She was skinny, no hips, and she needed some sun. Everything about her body language announced she was capable of pulling the trigger: her small feet were braced in the sand, her body locked in an aggressive position, her chin brazenly cocked.

He believed she was capable of shooting him until he really looked at her face. Her eyes were the color of blue shadows, bruise-dark and soft—spaniel-soft—and wild with anxiety. Strain pinched lines near her temples; chalk had more color than her face. She was scared, and not in a pretty way. She was sick with fear, panicked with fear, desperate with fear.

"Did you hear me?" she demanded. "I said to clear out. This is private land."

"I heard you."

His tone was a roasted marshmallow, soft from the inside out. A hunter's instincts warned him not to shake her any more than she was obviously shaken. She was biting her bottom lip raw. Both determination and anxiety blazed in her eyes.

His senses took in the backdrop of a sun-kissed morning, bird song, the lapping of waves and the scent of water and woods. It wasn't a morning for nightmares . . . but then this wasn't *his* nightmare. He seemed to have inadvertently walked into hers.

His mind didn't frame questions. Whys belonged in another place and time; thinking was an irrelevant luxury as long as she was holding the shotgun. Choices didn't take place in his head; they took place in his blood. The sharp, raw emotion slamming through him was unidentifiable, but it wasn't fear. She had enough fear for both of them. He knew because he never took his eyes off her face.

Carefully, casually, he said, "I didn't realize anyone lived on the island, as I was telling the boy. I have a cottage—cedar and glass, you can see it from the other side of the island. My name's Jarl Hendriks—"

He extended a hand. She obviously didn't expect his gesture, and didn't seem to know what to do about it. The gun barrel dropped several inches, and her eyes darted first to the woods, where the boy had disappeared, then back to him. In those short seconds when her gaze was fastened with fierce intensity on his face, he edged out of the water. Maybe she saw him move and maybe she didn't, but he never broke eye contact. It seemed to distract her.

He assumed she was evaluating his looks for threat potential, which was fine. He knew what she saw, which was nothing that had ever intimidated anyone.

He'd never reached six feet, and typical of his Finnish heritage had dark hair, dark eyes, and the clear, clean skin of a seagoing people. Nature had carved his face with bold

strokes—a square chin, jutting cheekbones, a strong brow—
but there was nothing in his looks to make a woman nervous. Stray animals followed him home. People he met for
the first time trusted him. People saw a worker in the wire-
wrapped muscles in his shoulders and arms. They saw a patient, responsible man of character in the road map of lines
in his face. They saw a man with dark, gentle eyes who
laughed easily.

There was another Jarl, of course, beneath the surface.
A few women—a very few—had discovered that he was a
creative and committed lover. No man had ever tried to
cross him twice. What he believed in he believed in fiercely,
from the gut, no backing down and no holds barred, but
that was no one's business but his own. Strength could be
measured in silence. A man didn't have to parade courage.

All of that was very nice but not immediately relevant.
What she could see to judge was what mattered, and he gave
her ample time to figure out that he wasn't remotely related
to a big bad bear. It didn't work. She focused, but didn't
see. She was too damn busy being panicked to see. Jarl took
another step, his open palm extended in an offer of a handshake.

"Don't come any closer! Please. We don't care for visitors. This is private land. I'm sorry if I seem inhospitable,
but that's the way it is, and I—" she suddenly stopped.

Her voice was hoarse, a rough-silk feminine alto, a voice
that would inevitably make a man think of satin sheets and
moonlight—another time. For now, though, enough was
enough.

With his right hand still outstretched, his left calmly
whipped out and snatched the gun. She made a small
sound—a trapped, wild sound—not unlike the despairing
pigeon he'd found the day before.

He paid no attention. As naturally as sun shines, he
started talking again. "Like I said, I live in a cottage across
the lake—fifteen acres—had the land for about three years."
Head bent, he flipped open the chamber, intending to re-
move the bullets, and discovered ruefully that there weren't

any. He should have guessed. "I'm here for a month's vacation. I own a hardware store north of Detroit. Anyway, I'll be around the lake for a while. If you want, I'll teach you how to load and use this."

"Pardon?"

"The shotgun. It isn't going to do you much good if you don't know what to do with it." He laid the gun on the shore, not where she could reach it, and not where the child could surprise him from the woods and grab it before he did. With or without bullets, a gun was a weapon.

When he straightened, he let out a long, low breath. A stunning sensation of rawness had cramped every muscle in his body. Until that instant he hadn't realized that the emotion knifing through him was anger—not a civilized man's dawdle with temper, but a caveman rage. He didn't need, ever again, to have a lethal weapon pointed at his head. For two cents he'd shake this woman until her teeth rattled for pulling such a damn fool stunt.

He didn't have the two cents, and when his gaze whipped toward her again, he couldn't hold on to the anger. Without a gun in her hands, she looked as vulnerable as a naked lover in bed. She certainly didn't realize that. Her chin was locked in a position of pride. Determination ruled her posture; she'd stuffed her shaky hands into her pockets, and her eyes met his squarely. She seemed to think she looked tough.

She looked about as tough as cobweb silk, and being a smart man, he had the sound instincts to take off faster than a bat out of hell. The woman obviously had problems—none of which were his business. Who needed it?

Somehow, though, instead of sprinting for his boat at sensible breakneck speed, he found himself trudging toward her again, as easily and slowly as he would have approached a wounded wild creature. "I caught the boy's name—Kip?—but not yours. You've got the same eyes. I take it he's your son?"

She ignored the question with an exasperated toss of her head. "Look, I'm aware I must not seem like the neighborly type, but I'm trying to make it as clear as I know how. We do not want or appreciate visitors. We—''

"You couldn't have been here long.'' He looked past her. Beyond the sumac and jungle growth of scrub, he could see the shadow of a large oak-and-maple-shaded building. Not a house, but maybe it had been a clubhouse once. The two-story sprawler was made of logs. Several windows were missing, and some were cracked. Broken shingles dangled from the roof. Weeds grew as high as the veranda that surrounded the place. "I hope it isn't just you and the boy taking over the island? You've bit off a lot of work. Raised homers long?''

"No."

His gaze drifted back to her. "It had to be your bird I saved yesterday.''

"I don't raise birds.''

She fibbed well. And the way her fingers dug into her front jeans pockets drew attention to her chest. It was a minimal-sized chest by Jarl's preferred standards, but there was something to be said for the long white throat and the way the soft red shirt draped the two small mounds of her breasts. She was built elegantly. She was built for soft summer winds, the sip of mint juleps, lazy flirtations and lace.

She looked no more complicated than a soft, gentle lady, except that he had no doubt whatsoever that she'd come at him with fingernail claws and teeth if he threatened her...or the boy. Maybe that was why he couldn't make himself leave. It was just a morning. He was just an innocent trespasser. This wasn't the inner city, a bed of criminal intrigue or a terrorist stronghold. This was a small, simple island. What had her so shook, so clutch-scared that she reacted to an ordinary stranger as if dragons were after her?

"I seemed to have startled the little boy,'' he admitted cheerfully. "I never meant to. Most kids take a look at me and figure out pretty quick that I'm not the kind of 'scary stranger' their mothers teach them to avoid.'' The double message was clear, but there was only one groove on the woman's record.

"Mr. Hendriks, please go away."

"Jarl," he corrected her amiably.

"You don't seem to be listening to me. Maybe I forgot to load the gun—"

He had to correct her. "You've never loaded a gun in your life."

"So maybe you got the impression I wasn't serious. I am very serious. I don't want you—or anyone—here. It's my island. No Trespassing signs are posted all over the place."

He nodded. "You have a functional generator?" He glanced around again. "No electrical or phone wires running to the island obviously. But it would be pretty rough camping out here for any period of time without a generator."

"Mr. Hendriks—"

"Jarl," he corrected her again, and reextended his hand. "Why don't we get this handshake over with? I still haven't caught your name."

Face flushed with exasperation, she spit out, "Sara." Quicker than an angry cat, she jerked her arm forward, clamped a hand in his and backed off. "You have your handshake. Now would you leave?"

Her palm had been small, soft and wet from nervousness and fear—never mind how cool and controlled she was trying to look. "There aren't more than a half-dozen cottages or homes around the lake. You're not likely to be bothered, but if you're worried about strangers, I'll keep an eye out for you now that I know you're on the island. And before you rush in and offer coffee, I'm afraid I can't stay. Trout won't bite much past dawn—but I'll be back to teach you about the gun."

"*No.*"

He didn't have more time to dawdle. He'd let go of the boat rope because of all this nonsense, and although his rowboat was grounded in the shallows, it was rocking. Five minutes from now he'd have to swim a mile back to shore whether he wanted to or not. "I'll bring you a trout dinner one of these nights if I can—but I'm making no promises.

The fish in this lake are fisherman-wary, smart about a hook no matter what's hiding it—''

''*No.*''

He climbed back into his boat and poled out slowly. ''Remember my cottage is the dark cedar. You can see it from the other side of the island. If you need any help—''

''*No.*''

If he listened to her limited vocabulary, he would undoubtedly have gotten the impression that he was unwanted.

The small country of Finland, however, had upheld its border with the giant, hostile and heavily armed Russia for centuries. No other country on earth now successfully coexisted with Russia against those kinds of odds. But the Finns had. The Finns had mastered some unique tricks of survival through those centuries: not only sheer, bloody stubbornness, but also the subtle and often annoying traits of endurance and tenacity.

He figured she wasn't quite in the mood to hear the history of his Finnish heritage. Her small frame grew smaller as his boat gained distance on the lake. The sun brought out red glints in her hair. Belatedly, he realized that she was lovely.

She never turned away for as long as he was within sight, as if to ensure he was definitely leaving. Her message—leave me alone—was projected for a quarter mile. Then a half mile. She was so small. He heard the mental voice begging him to let her be even when he rounded the bend at the oval curve of the island.

A restless, fretful summer wind picked up as he steered for home. The lake splashed up a diamondlike froth under the stroke of his oars. He caught the silver gleam of a trout and felt the sun baking through his flannel shirt. It was going to be hot, his stomach growled for breakfast, and it was suddenly that kind of morning again. Normal—sun, water, heat and hunger. A gull soared near shore, then screamed furiously when she missed her fish.

Another time he would have smiled. Not this morning.

She didn't want anyone near her or the child. That was clear, and Jarl never intruded where he wasn't wanted. He valued privacy and freedom. He never pushed a woman— ever, no exceptions. Maybe she had trouble. Maybe she didn't. It was none of his business. He didn't know her and he didn't have any reason to care.

Forgetting the whole incident was the wisest choice.

He resolved, immediately, to do just that.

Long after he was gone Sara stood frozen. Her fingertips were icy, her heart still thumped savage rhythms. Fear ran up and down her spine.

Sometime, somewhere, someone was going to find them. A hundred times she'd planned for that happening. She'd thought out exactly what she was going to say, how she would act, what she had to do.

She closed her eyes, feeling the squeeze of acid in her stomach. She hadn't done anything right. She'd taken one look at him and panicked like a goose. You have no room to make mistakes like that, Sara, she chastised herself. None. Stupid, stupid, stupid...

With a grimace she trudged over to the shotgun and picked it up with the same enthusiasm she'd show a snake. The darn gun was part of it. Max was the one who'd insisted she have it, and at the time she hadn't argued. She was as capable of playing the role of a female Rambo as a butterfly.

That's not good enough, Sara, her inner voice continued. What if he'd recognized you? What if he'd recognized Kip?

She moved then, fast, dodging a scratchy sumac branch and pushing through the brush. It took a few minutes to reach the shadowed veranda of their clubhouse-turned-home, and another few to lock the shotgun in the cabinet in her bedroom closet. Striding back outside, she called, "Kip!"

Like a present, he was suddenly there, gamboling out of the woods, a wrapped-up package of solemn eyes and sandy knees and hair going every which way. He was hugging the bulldozer he always carried, and Sara suddenly couldn't wait for him to reach her.

She swooped down on him and scooped him up, bulldozer and all. Skinny or not, he weighed a ton. He was also a dreadful squirmer. He smelled like milk, sandbox dirt and toothpaste. He smelled like love, like her son, like the only thing in the entire world that mattered.

She trailed big smacking-loud kisses on his cheek and neck. "I need your help, young man."

More kisses. A year ago he would have chortled in a big belly laugh at kisses like this. But then a year ago her four-year-old son hadn't known what hell was.

More kisses. More squirming, and his small, shy smile finally broke. She couldn't have been happier if she'd won mink and diamonds. "Hey. Are you going to help me, or are you just going to stand around all morning kissing me?"

"Mom! You're the one kissing *me*!"

"You're kidding!" It was easier to carry him around the side of the house than to let him down. Not easier on her muscles, just easier on her heart. She silently vowed, I'll have you laughing again. I'll have you safe. No one's ever going to hurt you again, Kip. No one. On my life.

Three cages of pigeons were nailed to the side of the house. The soft-winged birds cooed and fluttered when Sara and Kip drew near.

"It's not time to feed them," Kip reminded her.

"I know. We're going to let some fly, but I can't open the cage door all by myself."

"Mom! You can, too. It's easy!"

Sara shook her head. "I can't. It's just too tough for me."

It wasn't too tough for Kip. He flipped the metal switch on the cage, and there was another smile when his small hand poked in and stroked the velvet wing of his favorite. He loved the birds.

One by one the homers scuttled out of the cage. One perched on the roof, another at the cage rim, all talk-talk-talking in those throaty coos. Like fussy little men, they took their time getting organized, but ultimately they knew what their job was. The lead pigeon was named Harry—Kip had christened him—and when Harry soared for the sky, the others followed.

Both mother and son raised hands to their foreheads to shade the morning sun, watching the six wing free across the lake.

"They'll come back?" Kip worried.

He always asked the same thing. "They'll be back," she promised.

"I'd like to fly," he mused.

She smiled. "Me, too."

His forehead puckered in a frown. "Why did we let so many go all at once? We never do that."

She diverted Kip's attention with chatter about swimming and making cookies, but took one last look at the birds before herding her son into the house. Every day she sent three homers off to Max. Three gave him the message that they were all right, healthy and doing fine. If she or Kip were hurt, she would have communicated an SOS to Max by releasing all the birds.

A sending of six birds was middle ground. Max would understand that no one was hurt, no one was in danger, but that she wanted to see him when he had the time. A simple stranger wandering onto the island hardly justified total panic.

Except in her heart. Who was kidding who? She was scared out of her mind.

Two

Nothing erased nightmares faster than hard work, and four hours of physical labor was better than one. Sara stashed the hoe in the shed and latched the door.

Prickly heat itched her neck. Drops of perspiration tickled between her breasts. The two new blisters stung like fire, and she'd long stopped worrying about when Max was going to get there. Months ago she'd blithely assumed the human body had a few dozen muscles. Now she could testify to at least five hundred, each of which could independently creak and groan.

She'd probably sell her soul for a nice warm bath and some soothing lotion. As her gaze ruefully swept the freshly hoed garden, she changed that pact with the devil for brawn, calluses and a supply of physical stamina.

The garden looked fine, and their potential food supply was her obvious priority, but the leaks in the clubhouse roof couldn't be ignored much longer. The yard was half jungle. A veranda step was hanging. She could hear the ancient generator wheezing like a machine with T.B. And inside the house...no one but a masochist would list all the things that had to be immediately done to make the old clubhouse into a home.

Three solid weeks of physical labor hadn't begun to dent her critical-priority list. On the other hand, she was a long way from Oriental carpets, Limoges china and a mansion in Grosse Pointe, which was solace of a kind.

Sucking on the hottest blister, she crossed the yard to the shade of an old elm and leaned against the gnarled bark. Weary muscles eased as she watched her son *vroom vroom* with his bulldozer.

Maybe because of their long morning swim she'd been able to con Kip into a nap after lunch. Midafternoon, though, was rigidly scheduled as tunnel-digging time. From the beginning Kip had claimed the west corner of the yard, and his current project was a very serious business, judging by the vocal level of the *vrooms*. Sara smiled. Dirt had a way of flying at Kip. The only thing on her son not gray was his grave blue eyes.

He was concentrating when he suddenly snatched his bulldozer and crashed for the woods. If she'd heard no sound to explain his bolting, she knew her son. She straightened automatically, her gaze turning to the path that led to the lake dock.

Seconds later Max appeared, carrying a giant box, the familiar chewed-off cigar clamped between his teeth. An old T-shirt accented the double roll around his beer belly. Iron-gray whiskers covered his ruddy face; a snake tattoo climbed up his upper arm and a scar sliced his right eyebrow in two parts. Even if he was given a tux and a limo, Max still wouldn't look reputable.

Sara surged toward him with an open smile. "Do you have more for me to bring up from the boat?"

"I'll get the stuff in a minute." He jammed the box down on the veranda and swiped a forearm at his damp forehead. Hard blue eyes swept possessively over her face. "It was supply day, anyhow. You didn't need to send the extra pigeons."

"I didn't send them to remind you about the supplies, but that'll wait until we get inside." Her head tilted in the direction of the woods, a gesture Max understood. She didn't want to talk where Kip could conceivably hear.

He nodded, squinting at the small figure hiding in the shadow of a tree. "He's all right?"

"Better every day."

"Swimming lessons going okay?" He always asked that same question because he liked to watch her emanate pride.

"I think he'll be going for the Olympics by the time he's six. He can already swim the circumference of the island."

"Yeah? And he's a fast tyke—took off like a bat out of hell when he saw me coming. Dammit, Sara, you think he'd be used to me by now."

Her voice softened. "It's not you, Max. It's any man. It's just going to take him some time. He can't help it."

"Yeah, yeah. Maybe he'll come around when I carry the pigeons up. I got the birds, food, supplies to bring up from the boat—also the order for that fancy paper and paints you wanted. But that'll all wait, and so will whatever you got to tell me." Gruff and testy, he insisted she open the box, and then stood there looking bored when Sara obediently flipped the cardboard flaps.

"You sweetheart! Crayons and a coloring book."

Max flushed dark as red leather. "Look in the bottom there. There's something for you, too."

For his sake, she took the time to forage for the tiny vial. She unscrewed the top, took a whiff and discovered the most atrociously strong dime store toilet water that her nose had ever come across. "Ah, Max..." She threw her arms around him and bussed his cheek. "You're a darling, you know that?"

"Yeah, yeah. Figured you needed a little pick-me-up. Actually I figured you'd rather have something like lipstick, but there's no way I could buy a woman lipstick, and that stuff smelled so good."

"It's wonderful," she assured him.

"Yeah. I knew you'd like it." Max rolled his shoulders. "Let's get this show on the road."

The last thing he hauled from the boat was a beer. He didn't pop the top until he was settled at the scarred pine table in the kitchen, and he hadn't had the chance to swallow the first swig before Sara asked abruptly, "What was in the papers?"

Once the tyke was out of hearing range, he should have expected the question. "Crime, trouble in the Middle East." At the look on her face, he sighed. "Yeah, they're still running the pictures, but less than they were. The one of your ex-husband looks like a saint."

"All the Chapmans look like saints," Sara said wryly.

"My best guess is that money's changing hands to keep those pictures in the news. If it were anybody but a Chapman, any public interest would have faded a long time ago." He chugged half the can in three gulps, watching her. "You can quit unpacking—that'll wait until tonight. And you can quit jumping over to that window—the tyke's fine. He ain't going anywhere he shouldn't, which you know. It's half a miracle he's let you out of his sight as it is. You look worn out and you look antsy and you look shook up. Now what happened?"

"Nothing worth worrying you about. I knew the minute I sent off the pigeons that doing it was a mistake—"

"You gonna dither or you gonna talk?"

She took a breath. "Someone found us this morning. A man, a stranger, came on the island."

"And upset you to beat the band," Max said shrewdly.

Her smile was dry. "We're talking knocking knees, thundering heartbeat, whipped nerves. A classic case of stupidity and no excuses."

"Honey, God'd be scared if he were sitting in your shoes but get on with it. What was he doing here? Did he recognize you? What'd he look like? Who was he?"

Sara had been over the same questions a hundred times in her mind since that morning. "I'm as positive as I can be that he didn't know who we were. He seemed too surprised to find anyone on the island, and he never said or looked or did anything to make me think he'd ever seen a picture of us."

She'd been waiting to tell it all to Max, yet she found herself hesitating. Scant seconds passed, in which she focused blindly on the red checked curtains, the pitted red linoleum floor, the cracked porcelain sink and the relic of a cooking stove. She saw none of it. She only saw him, the stranger, as sure and real as if he were standing there. "As far as what he looked like, I'd guess early thirties. Not as tall as six feet, but close. Lean, muscular, a physical build. Dark hair, dark eyes..."

The words easily tripped out for Max, but said aloud, she knew they weren't right. Anything she said made the stranger sound innocuous-looking. He hadn't been innocuous-looking. This morning, panic and anxiety had so dominated her mind that his physical appearance had barely registered. Now she could remember what mattered, but she couldn't find a way to express it.

He'd had dark eyes, old eyes, gentle eyes. How could she explain that to Max? And Kip bolted whenever a man—any man—came near him. Kip hadn't bolted when the stranger talked to him, but Max would hardly believe her if she told him.

"He said he was a neighbor, owned a cottage across the lake. I think all he originally intended was to explore the island out of curiosity."

She remembered his curiosity too clearly, not only as a memory but also as an emotion that sent her pulse vibrating. Even with the gun pointed at him, he hadn't been shaken. She'd been mean and nasty and unfriendly, but he'd just kept looking at her, talking to her, in that soothing, low baritone. "He had an accent," she recalled distractedly. "Not something pronounced or heavy, but it was definitely there, a soft sound in the way he said certain words."

"Ah, the Finn. Jarl Hendriks."

"That was the name. You know him?"

"Sure, I know him. He gasses up his boat at the bait shop. A man's man, that one. Never seen anybody around his place but him. Put up that cottage board by board alone." Max's fingers drummed over his stomach. He started to say something, then substituted a thoughtful "How'd you handle him?"

"Like a blithering idiot," she said dryly.

"And the pope turned Jewish."

She didn't smile. "I mean it. It's not that I didn't know it was going to happen. I can't remember a summer when some kid or cottager didn't get curious and row out here to explore. I knew it was going to happen sometime, and I was prepared—in my head. I just wasn't prepared for my knees to start knocking when I saw him."

"You got more guts than any three men I know, honey. And there's no reason anybody'd link you with the lady in the Detroit papers unless you let on."

"I know that."

"Your hair's short, nothing like it used to be. You don't look anything like those pictures, anyhow."

"I know," she repeated.

"What I know of him, Hendriks is the kind to mind his own business. Better him than someone else." He watched her nod, but her eyes still looked haunted and lost. Abruptly, he changed tactics. "All right. We could move you and Kip. Where I don't know, but we could do that. But if one day you're on the island and next day you're not, well . . . if he *wasn't* curious, Sara, sure seems like that'd be a good way to make him suddenly curious."

"I know," Sara echoed for the third time. She'd already come to the same conclusions. And where could they move where there was absolutely no chance of running into another human being? The Arctic?

Max's eyes turned colder than blue steel. "He make any kind of move toward you or the boy?"

"No, it was nothing like that. *He* was nothing like that."

"Sure?"

Once panic stopped clouding her judgment, she knew her instincts were right. "Dead sure."

Max's fingers went back to their drumming. "So I hate to suggest it, but we might as well relax. Ain't nothing we're going to do, ain't nothing we need to do, ain't nothing we can do. A man got curious and said hello. If I was twenty years younger and caught a look at you, I'd get curious and say hello, too. If he comes back, you practice boring him to death. Somebody else comes around, you bore them, too, with how natural and ordinary you are. You got other choices I don't know about? Course we do got other choices. We can sit here and panic till the cows come home. Panic sure does help. You want to sit here and work yourself up into a heart attack, I guess I'll just sit here and work up to a heart attack with you. I—"

"Oh, shut up, Max. And I'm sorry I worried you by sending off the pigeons." She marched over and plopped a kiss on his bald spot, which immediately turned brick red. Blood was still pumping anxiety through her veins, but Max didn't need to know it. She'd burdened him enough with her problems. "Thanks for coming," she said softly. "From the beginning, I don't know what the two of us would have done without you. I owe you more than thanks—"

"Cripes, don't start *that* junk."

He looked a cross between disgusted and horrified. She wagged a finger at him. "I'll thank you if I want to thank you, you old coot, and if you light that cigar—"

He stashed the chewed-off cigar back into his pocket. "It was my first one of the day," he said balefully.

"And it's New Year's Eve."

They bickered fast and hard while she finished stacking the canned goods from the boxes. He loved being teased. She showed no mercy. She'd known Max ever since he'd rented a cottage to her parents when she was a child. Way back then she'd been an innocent girl in pigtails. He'd been a jailhound, whiskered coot who spoke in snarls and swear words.

Lord knew how a kinship had developed, but even after her parents died, Sara had made a regular habit of dropping in on him. No one else seemed to care about him. No one else seemed to argue with him. There had been no one else to sit with him when he'd been laid up with a broken leg after a car accident.

Sara had other relatives, including a sister and brother, but there was no one but Max who she could conceivably turn to for the kind of trouble she was in. Max hadn't just come through. He'd gone out on a giant limb for her.

Halfway through her unpacking, she stopped to press two fingers against the angry headache in her temples. When she was an eleven-year-old pigtailed kid, it had never occurred to her that she could conceivably end up a fugitive, hiding out on an island, wanted by the police. Or that stories about her being an unfit, abusive mother would be plastered across the newspapers.

Max had been waiting for her fake chatter to lose momentum. "Things'll come out right, Sara. You'll see."

"Of course they will," she said immediately, but the stranger that morning had reminded her of the real truth. Fear was real. So was despair. Nothing in her life had a prayer of turning out right again.

Except for Kip.

About a million years ago her parents had taught her how to love, how to give, the value of gentleness and serenity. Ugly emotions—like rage and hate—had never been part of her life. Until her son was threatened.

A woman, she'd discovered, could be absolutely anything she had to be. A mother's instincts had the power to transcend every civilized value, principle and law. When need be, even a tame, gentle woman could turn into a lioness.

No one was going to hurt Kip again. No one. Ever. She'd see them in hell first.

By the time Jarl tugged his boat up on the island shore, he knew he had an audience. Without glancing toward the woods, he plucked the whittled crane from the bottom of the boat, set it on the sand, then left it.

Pushing up his plaid shirtsleeves, he grabbed his tool kit. Fifteen minutes later he had pried the four rotten boards from her dock. Late afternoon sun peppered the lake with white sparkles. A bare breeze puffed by, but it was hot.

Throwing off his shirt, he was aware the lad had found the courage to move closer—about five feet away from the toy crane. From the state of his untied hightops to a smudge of dirt on his cheek, Jarl could see the boy had obviously had a heavy play day. No smile, but the look he plastered on the crane was the unmistakable lust of a four-year-old.

"The crane's for you," Jarl affirmed without glancing up. "It's not as fancy as Fisher-Price, mind you, but it'll pick up some good-sized stones. You can have it, but you have to ask your mom first. Never take anything from a stranger without asking your mom, right?"

Jarl didn't wait for an answer. Back still turned from the boy, he started hauling cedar boards and a handsaw from the boat. The boards had been precut at home—most docks were of a similar size—but they needed trimming to fit. He had the four in place and was standing in ankle-deep water with a hammer in his hand when Sara appeared from the woods path.

For four solid days he'd tried to forget her. Finns excelled at avoiding trouble. Who needed the grief? And at first glance she sure didn't look like a woman who could ransom a man's common sense.

Her skin had a little more sun-kissed color than it had shown four days ago, but that was neither here nor there. White paint flecked her cheek and her hair had been pulled back with a boldly printed scarf. Her jeans were loose; her big blue shirt drowned what figure she had. He liked a woman with hips and a few more curves. Sara had neither.

This time she wasn't looking wild and she wasn't toting a gun, but she had other weapons to rattle a man: the dance of freckles across her nose; the soft red mouth; shoulders squared with sassy arrogance. She really believed she could tackle a bear this time, and the courage in her eyes made his own soften.

"*Mr.* Hendriks, what on earth do you think you're doing?"

It was perfectly obvious what he was doing, but he catered to her. "Fixing your dock." He set the first nail with a tap, drilling it in true and reached for another one.

"I can fix my own dock! You can't just walk onto someone's private property and—"

"I know." Jarl's voice was rueful. He didn't look up. "Fact is, I was going nuts with nothing to do." *Tap, drill. Tap, drill.* "See, I scheduled this month's vacation for myself. Seemed like a good idea. I haven't taken more than weekends off in years, but look at my place across the lake. There's a two-story greenhouse atrium. Not a plant in it needs watering. No weeds left to pull in the yard. I built the darn cottage out of cedar, which means I'll never have any decent upkeep projects to do on it. A man can only fish and sauna so many hours—"

"None of that is my problem! I don't want you to do this."

He continued to hammer. "It's not that I don't like solitude. I do. I work with people all day. By night I walk alone, read alone, sauna alone. And like it. Can't say I always like to sleep alone."

"Mr. Hendriks—"

Tap, drill. Tap, drill. "But then I'm fussy about sharing a bed. Always have been, and big, bold aggressive women are the kind that appeal to me. Blond, not brunette. Brown eyes, never blue. Never once went for a woman in a blue blouse, and I hate scarves." He straightened, glanced at her and blinked as if in stunned surprise at her appearance. "I guess it's a cinch you're safe as church," he said mildly, "so I can't imagine what possible harm it would be for me to fix your dock."

Her jaw dropped, then she clamped it closed. He noticed that she nearly forgot herself and chuckled, but then she propped her hands on her hips and practiced looking tough again. "Mr. Hendriks—"

"Could have sworn I told you my first name was Jarl. You going to keep the boy waiting until Christmas before letting on he can have the crane?"

Her blustering and flustering ceased when she neared the toy. By then the little one had stolen close and locked his hand in hers. The bond between mother and son was so bright and strong that it made the sun pale. Strain dropped from her shoulders when she looked at the boy. The tight lines around her eyes vanished. The loving look she gave Kip took her face beyond beauty; it damn near stole the air from his lungs.

Her fingers skimmed the smooth wood of the crane, the intricate little pulley, the wood-burned Kip on the side. When she glanced at Jarl again, she looked as helpless as a snowflake in a thaw: meltable, helpless, fragile. "You made this yourself?"

"It's no big thing. I work with wood as a hobby."

"You shouldn't have. I don't know how to thank you."

"That's not your problem. It's his. As far as I can tell, that turns into Kip's crane just as soon as he gives me a thank-you."

Immediately she shook her head. "It's not that he wouldn't be grateful, but I'm afraid my son can't—"

"THANK YOU!"

"—talk."

She didn't see the expression on Jarl's face. She was too busy looking at her son with shock. Her eyes flew from Kip to Jarl and back again. The little one whisked Jarl a smile— so big it split his whole face—and then bundled the huge crane close to his chest and took off.

The mother looked as if she wanted to take off as well. She straightened and said briskly, "The crane was kind of you. Terribly kind. But—"

"The dock's sturdy again, although it'll look like the devil until you get a coat of paint on it." He piled the tools back in the kit. "Sure could use a drink. Lemonade, iced tea…"

She stared at all the work he'd done, then sighed uneasily. "All right. I'll bring you a drink from the house. You just stay right here. I'll bring it down."

He nodded.

"Stay here," she repeated.

He nodded again, and then as soon as she turned, waded out of the water and followed her. She didn't realize he was right behind her until she'd forged ahead a good five feet. "Jarl!"

His first name wasn't just another four-letter word. Someday he'd have to tell her that. "You must have been painting. You've got white on your chin. How bad a shape is the old building in?"

"The building, the property, the dock and the grounds are *my* problem. I don't want help. I appreciate the crane you made for Kip, but I don't need help."

She could specialize in being a nonwelcoming committee of one. He gently patted her shoulder, a consoling gesture, and moved past her. The tangled brush that surrounded the island made for a natural privacy barrier. He guessed the land had been let go for just that purpose.

Once inside the clearing, Jarl could see that there were several acres she had clearly been trying to recivilize. Waist-high weeds dominated the peach orchard at the far end, but the gold-pink balls on the trees promised a crop in another few weeks. Her garden had been freshly hoed. Walnut and maple woods clustered at the east end of the property, which was carpeted with native trillium and wild violets. Sumac was trying to take over the edge; she'd hacked away half of it. She'd also tackled half the calf-high lawn with a rusty hand mower that was standing in the shade of the veranda.

"You're not coming in the house," she said firmly.

"No," he agreed, as if the idea appalled him.

"I'm painting in the kitchen. You have to go right after this. I don't mind getting you a drink, but—"

"Thanks, I appreciate it."

When she disappeared beyond the banging screen door, he studied her place. Shingles dangled from the roof like drunken sailors; he could count the potential leaks. Nobody had rechinked between the logs in years. The metal casement windows were going to be salvageable only if they got treated to primer and paint soon. Still, the overall log structure appeared sound. There wasn't anything that a dozen men and some decent equipment couldn't fix in a few weeks' time.

She came out with a glass wrapped in a napkin, and when she handed it to him, he had a quick glimpse of the blisters on her soft white hand. The look of those blisters sent his pulse thrumming, the cords in his neck tightening.

He forced a gulp of the tangy-sweet lemonade down his dry throat. Leaning back against the veranda rail, he sipped the rest with deliberate slowness. She obviously wasn't going to budge from her guard post in front of the door.

"You have space for a sauna, right about there." He motioned to the spot just beyond the porch.

"A sauna!" For the first time he caught a look of humor in her eyes. "I've got a few other priorities on this place before I worry about luxuries."

"Luxuries?" He tested the word on his tongue. "Americans have different priorities than Finns. The poorest man in Finland would build his sauna before he tackled the building of any other shelter. A Finnish sauna, of course, is drastically different than the American kind."

"I take it you're from Fin—" Quickly, she cut herself off. "You must be nearly done with that drink."

He nodded but answered the question she'd nearly asked. "I'm an American citizen now, but I was born in Finland, emigrated when I was eighteen. I had lost both my parents, came over here as an orphan."

"So young?" she murmured, and then caught her breath again. "Mr. Hendriks—"

"Jarl."

"Jarl, then. You've finished the drink," she said pointedly.

"Your son has your eyes, your hair color. Built more like a reed than an oak, isn't he? But healthy. Strong in his own way.'' His gaze squinted toward the corner of the yard where the little one was putting the crane and bulldozer to heavy use. When Jarl lifted his head, he saw her attention had been diverted to her son.

Fierce and soft. The words should not normally have been paired, but they did in her eyes. The woman with the cameo profile had something of a lioness in her. The love she felt for her son was fierce, huge, and as naked as her small red mouth.

Jarl had no illusions that she'd only let him get this far because of the crane he'd made the boy. It didn't take a mind reader to figure out she would deny the little one nothing. Nor, he guessed, would she deny the right lover anything, because a woman with that kind of emotion and passion would be helpless to do otherwise.

The thought clung to his imagination like a cobweb in a corner—unwanted and annoying—but tenacious.

Her gaze whipped back to him. ''Jarl—''

''As much as I've enjoyed our little talk, I have to be going,'' he said regretfully, setting the glass on the steps and lurching to his feet. ''Kip!''

The little one looked up.

''You figured out how the pulley works on the crane?''

''Sure.''

Again he felt Sara's eyes riveted on him. ''Okeydoke. Catch you later.'' He turned to Sara. ''Thanks for the drink,'' he said, and strode toward the woods. He could feel two sets of eyes boring into his back like the heat of the sun until he was out of sight.

At the dock he still had tools and a tool kit to stash before he could take off. He did that and was just pushing the boat back into the water when Sara appeared through the brush, holding her arms tight, her head high. ''I didn't thank you for the dock and the crane.''

''Sure you did.''

''But I have to ask you not to come again.''

He figured she had to make that one last stab at ensuring he didn't return. "Like I told you, I'll bring you a trout dinner when I can."

"This is private property. If you come again, I'll have to..." She took a huge breath. "I'll have to take some kind of action. Legal action."

For the sake of her pride, he didn't let on how silly she sounded. "You ever had Lakka?"

"Lakka?"

"A liqueur made from cloudberries. I'll bring it when I come the next time, too."

"Do you hear me? No! You *can't* come back here," she repeated.

But because she sounded so desperate he knew he'd be back. And this time he doubted he'd be able to wait four days.

Three

The crane shared Kip's seat at dinner, was propped between his feet when he fed the homers and was held in his arms when he listened to a bedtime story about Bert and Ernie and bottlecaps. Sara drew the line when it came down to sleeping with it.

"It can't sleep without me," Kip insisted.

"It'll be waiting to play with you first thing in the morning, punkin."

"And it's too early to go to sleep."

To distract him she chased him up the stairs and swung him up high in her arms halfway down the hall. "I need a thousand kisses before you can sleep," she warned him.

"Mush."

He wriggled like an eel, but then he clung, arms tight at her neck, smiles suddenly gone. He dreaded bedtimes.

Deliberately she started humming as she pulled off his T-shirt and jeans. By the time he was washed and in pajamas, she began all the nighttime rituals: she looked under the bed for monsters, checked the closet for dragons, peeked behind the chest of drawers for alligators. Each time, she called out cheerfully when she found nothing. Each time, she only wished that Kip's fears were as simple as monsters, dragons and alligators.

After lighting the lamp, she tucked him into the bottom bunk bed. He had the smallest bedroom, the one next to hers and closest to the bathroom. The only rug she owned was by his bed, a bright throw rug in reds and blues. To make up for the sparse furniture, she'd hung pictures she'd done all over his walls; an oil of three doves; a charcoal of a rainbow; a penciled sketch of Big Bird; and his favorite, a watercolor of his bulldozer.

"Say good-night to Big Bird."

"Good night, Big Bird."

"Say good-night to the rainbow."

"Good night, Rainbow..."

But when it was all done his blue eyes shimmered with tears. "Don't leave me, Mom."

Her lips brushed his cheek and she hugged him. "You're right. We need one more quick story," she said calmly. After that she relented and brought up the crane, as Kip had undoubtedly known she would, as Sara had probably known she would, too. But when that was done she heard the same plaintive, "Mom, don't leave me!"

She wanted to stay. It would be so easy to climb into bed with her son and cuddle him until kingdom come. But that would have been for her sake, not her son's. Kip had to know she'd be there when he called, that she wasn't going to disappear on him again. To prove that meant having to leave him now.

Still, by the time she wandered into the stone-and-log living room, her eyes were stinging. Foolishness, really. In spite of all the desperate pleas, Kip always dropped off to sleep in seconds. Later, the nightmares would come. Those she could only deal with when they happened.

She stalled in the open door for a few moments. Outside, crickets and frogs had begun the night's symphony, and the sky was a marvelous royal blue, the horizon drenched in

jewel colors. Peace, solitude, silence. The island abounded
with all three at this time of night.

So relax, Sara, her inner voice chided. Imagination, not
reality, stirred her nerves. There was no dark-haired man
striding toward her through the dusk. She was alone and
safe, and so was her son.

The easel was standing empty at the corner of the living
room. She pulled a man's shirt over her clothes, turned up
the lamps and resolutely opened tubes of paint.

But Jarl shouldn't have come back. She'd been as rude
and cold and horrible as she knew how to be. What did it
take to discourage the man? In her imagination she could
still see the steady beat in his dark eyes. His voice was low,
his slight accent the hint of the erotic. That voice was a
gentle bass when he talked to Kip. It was a bass with spice
when he talked to her.

A few bold strokes of orange and blue, and a dragon took
shape on her paper. Not a fire-breathing dragon, but a
dragon that breathed diamonds and emeralds and rubies, as
befitted a fairy tale for a child. She painted his clawed toe-
nails peach. This was a vain dragon. Little ones didn't need
scary creatures. Real life had enough of them as it was.

At least try to relax, she told herself. Jarl was no dangerous dragon. He was just a man, and he'd shown a kindness
and sensitivity to Kip that had won a response from her son.
That was the only reason she couldn't forget him. How
could she continue to be mean to the first man who'd dented
Kip's defensive shell?

An hour later the first illustration was completed and she
started a second. The protagonist dragon in the children's
story was a patchwork of seal-brown, saffron and salmon.
He had a terrible inferiority complex. She knew exactly how
she wanted him to look, yet her brush slashed instead of
stroked, drew shaky lines instead of bold ones.

She crumpled the paper and gave up. Impatiently closing
tubes and gathering brushes, she stalked for the kitchen and
the turpentine. The acrid chemical stung the blisters on her
hands. The kerosene lantern flickered lonely shadows from

the window, and the dark, silent corners of the kitchen seemed to haunt her. Some nights she seemed as foolishly afraid of the dark as Kip was.

Only tonight it wasn't the darkness she was afraid of. It was him. Jarl. The man who'd won an impossible smile from her son, the man who made her pulse gambol like a frisky colt, the man with an exhausting, stubborn streak. She closed her eyes and saw his sun-weathered face, the lazy smile that nothing seemed to repress, the width of muscled shoulders that could make a woman believe he could protect her from life's real dragons.

Stop it, Sara! She opened her eyes, her throat dry, her heart aching. Protect her? What a joke. No human being, much less a lone man, could protect her when the entire legal system had failed.

Seven months ago she'd attended the custody hearing blithely armed with the truth and expecting justice. She'd been so naive! Divorce cases weren't about justice; they were about money. Attorneys made money based on the settlements they won for their clients. Nothing she had to say could compete with the Chapman fortunes and power. No one had cared that one small boy was shrapnel in the war.

Even when she lost custody she'd still fought for seven long months "the right way"—through the legal system, attorneys and Friend of the Court. All that time, Kip had had to believe she'd deserted him. All that time she'd wasted because she'd been stupid enough to believe someone would listen to the truth.

No one had, and four weeks ago she'd stolen her son. There had been no other way that she saw to save his life. She had no regrets, no guilt . . . except for waiting as long as necessary to do what had to be done.

She switched off the lamps in the kitchen, but instead of moving, found herself counting the dust motes in the darkness, listening to the silence, too afraid to go to sleep yet too exhausted to think.

At night her mind inevitably worked overtime. Kip was safe, and for now that was all that mattered, but the future loomed like an abyss. What would happen when he needed a doctor, a dentist? Her education had been in advertising, and sure, she'd sold some children's book illustrations. But could she make a living at it? What on earth was she going to do about schooling next year? All she wanted was to give her son a normal life, but for that he needed playmates, ice-cream cones, music, bikes. And her heart froze every time she thought of Kip getting ill.

Wearily she kneaded the tight muscle in her neck. "Don't think about it" was becoming her favorite song. Living minute-to-minute had become her life-style. The future held insurmountable problems, so she blocked thinking about them. Was there a choice? The only choice she'd never take was risking her son within the system again.

For the dozenth time that night Jarl's face sneaked into her thoughts. He was one of those "insurmountables." She should have realized four days ago that greeting him with a shotgun and hyperpanic was a foolish waste of energy. From the moment he'd stepped foot on the island, the damage was already done, the danger unerasable.

Maybe he hadn't already run across a picture of them in the media. When and if he did, though, he now knew what they looked like. That bridge was burned and she had no way to rebuild it. She had no other islands to run to. There was only one Max in her life. The only real protection she ever had was to live anonymously, innocuously, to be the kind of woman who aroused no one's suspicions or interest.

Jarl posed a nerve-racking catch-22. If he showed up again, she had to get rid of him. Only if he did show up again, she didn't dare raise too much fuss. She needed to arouse no more curiosity than she already had. She needed to come across as a normal single parent who was naturally wary of strangers because she was alone. She needed . . .

The word hovered like the lash of a whip in her mind. Needed? What she needed no longer had any possible bearing on her life. Kip's needs were all that mattered, all that could matter.

She straightened and headed for the stairs. Moonlight silvered through the windows in long, lonely waves. The wind had a wistful keen. And this night—like all nights now—was going to take an endless time to pass.

Jules Verne must have invented the island's rusty, creaky, monstrous-looking generator. Sara lifted her wrench, closed her eyes and offered a thousand virgin sacrifices to the gods that made generators good-tempered. She restarted it. The monster coughed once, but at least it didn't shake and its wheeze was gone. It worked—okay, only temporarily—but who ever said she was a plumber?

And her plumber's hands were full of grease. Humming, she used her elbow to push open the kitchen screen door and headed for the sink. Outside, a breeze rustled the branches of the huge maples and oaks. A nasty hot wind had been blowing off the lake all day, undoubtedly bringing in a storm. Amid the wind, the *buzz-humm* of the generator and the gush of running water on her hands, she almost missed a different kind of sound.

Quickly, she flipped off the faucets, and there it was again—Kip's chortle of laughter. Her heart swelled up so huge she couldn't breathe for a minute.

Nothing beat that sound. Nothing. Kip used to be famous for his irrepressible belly laugh, but not anymore. At least he was no longer mute, not with her, and he no longer closed up, withdrew into silence and sadness as he had when they'd first arrived here. Nightmares, though, still dominated his sleep, and wooing smiles and laughter from him were all uphill work. She hadn't heard her son's peal of innocent laughter—real laughter—in months.

Snatching a dish towel, she dashed outside and down the veranda steps, her lips parted to call his name. They closed rather abruptly. Kip was lying on his stomach in the grass, bare feet wagging in the air, and he was still chuckling. But he wasn't alone.

Jarl was also lying fanny-up and wearing jeans, nothing more. Dappled sun speckled the strong muscles of his shoulders and spine. His dark hair was disheveled, and he had his chin cocked in the palm of one hand. The two of them had a huge painted turtle trapped between them and Kip's sand tunnel. The turtle had traveled as far as Kip's arm and had its head raised, as if to say, "Look, you guys. Where's the way out?"

Her hands didn't want to release the towel, although her palms were abruptly desert-dry. All her good sense teetered on a shimmering wave of helplessness. Yes, she saw Jarl, and yes, she tried hard to arrange her face into a cold, rejecting expression. Only Kip was laughing. *Laughing*. Because of him.

"Mom!" The instant Kip spotted her he sprang to his feet. "Lookit! Isn't he wonderful?"

"Breathtaking," Sara agreed.

"Guess what?"

"What?"

"He's mine. All mine, if you say okay. And you have to say okay because he's for my birthday."

"Sweetheart, your birthday isn't for another eight months."

"But that's because I'm 'Merican. Jarl says I can be a..."

"Honorary." The word was supplied from the background.

"'Norary Finn," Kip continued. "Finns get two birthdays. Jarl said. One for a birthday and one for a..."

"Name day." Another contribution from the background.

"So Jarl says this can be my name day, which means I *have* to keep the turtle. I have to, Mom. He loves me. And I've already named him Poika. *Poika*'s a Finn word for *boy*. Jarl says... omigosh!"

When Kip had moved, the turtle had found a route to freedom. Legs flying, her son rushed back to reclaim it.

The last time Sara had heard Kip talk that fast, that hard, had been more than a year ago. Her gaze flew to the man responsible.

Jarl lay stretched out, a blade of grass between his teeth and a glint of humor in his grin. With lazy thoroughness, his gaze appraised the haphazard tie of her shirt at her midriff, the wild toss of her hair in the wind, the innocence in her joyful smile.

By the time his eyes pinned hers, Sara's smile was fading and a wayward sensation of softness was easing through her bloodstream. She'd felt trapped before, but not like this. The pep talk she'd given herself last night was worth as much as a pile of old newspapers. Treating this man as an enemy wasn't possible. His eyes were too beguiling, too full of laughter. His grin was irrepressibly sassy, and her son . . . She'd have sold her soul to anyone who could make her son laugh with such innocence and freedom again.

Still, she did her absolute best to make her voice sound exhaustively dismissive, vexed, weary. "So you're back, Mr. Hendriks."

Her inflection seemed to fly right by him. He simply nodded. "I told you I would be—when I had enough trout for a dinner. And Lakka—I told you I'd bring you a bottle of Lakka to try."

"You can't stay for dinner," she told him firmly.

"I won't," he agreed.

He lied. He did stay for dinner, but it wasn't her fault. He was like a stray cat: she couldn't catch him long enough to throw him out.

Kip never left Jarl's side when he cleaned and filleted the fish. Then the two paired up to collect driftwood for a beach fire. When the fire was blazing, her son insisted on showing Jarl his homers—how could she reasonably object to that?—and in the scant five minutes they were out of sight, they discussed building a sauna for her. Helpful as you please, Jarl volunteered to start on the project while she and Kip ate dinner. Good Lord! The last thing she wanted or needed on this earth was a sauna, and somehow because she didn't want a sauna he ended up eating with them.

When the last plate was scraped, Kip sat with knees bent and toes curled in the sand, mimicking exactly how she sat and as quiet as she was. Unlike her son, though, Sara studied her impossible neighbor over the fat yellow coals with ruthless intensity.

By then, restless little waves lapped at the shore. Clouds scuttled across a deepening blue sky. A storm was coming, and the water and sky and half-wild island suited Jarl too darn well.

The owner of a hardware store should look stable, practical, no-nonsense steady, and from his big strong hands to the gentle, whiskey-brown eyes, Jarl looked the part. His smile was as warm as the earth. He moved with the lazy assurance of a man who liked being a man. The wind kept rearranging an innocent, boyish lock of hair on his brow, but Sara wasn't fooled.

He wasn't tame. He wasn't civilized. He knew all the subtle, nasty, sneaky weapons of guerrilla warfare. He didn't argue and he didn't listen. He'd mowed through her discouraging greetings and stolen into their lives, and damn him, he had magic. There was no way on this earth she could trust him, but he had a way of looking at a woman that turned her insides to mush. Damn those beguiling, trust-me eyes! she thought. And he's had the dangerous perception to find the one, the only, weakness that made it impossible for Sara to be smart. He'd won over her son.

You're dangerous, Mr. Hendriks, Sara mused to herself. I'd rather handle a bomb than you. I'd rather be caught in a hurricane. I'd know what to do in a hurricane, but you...

Her eyes squeezed closed for a bare second, yet when she reopened them Jarl had leaned forward and lifted her glass from the sand. "You haven't tried the Lakka yet."

She shook her head. "I'm sorry. I don't drink."

But he patiently dangled the glass in midair, as if intending to hold it that way for the next four years. "How could a sip hurt you? I just want you to know what it tastes like."

Will you go away if I take a sip? When she took the drink, his hand brushed hers. His fingers were long, warm, brown. The short-lived physical contact was more tickle than substance, but it was enough. He was a man. Of course, so was

Max, but her pulse didn't slide down a long steep hill when Max accidentally touched her. "Do you read?" she asked abruptly.

"Read?" He obviously hadn't expected the question. "Sure. Fiction, mostly. Parker and MacDonald for fun, but sometimes the old American classics. I'm just discovering your Steinbeck, your Faulkner."

"You like fiction then, more than you like, say, journalism?"

"You mean newspapers? I subscribe to an investment journal, but no papers." Knees raised, his bare feet buried in the cooling sand, he finished the last of his wine. Part of his vision automatically took in the boy, playing a short distance away on the shore. Then all of his concentration centered on Sara, and he spoke slowly, finding his way. "Generally, papers are full of crime, politics, sensational stories. Nothing I know about, nothing I wish to be involved with. Maybe that comes from being raised in another country. That's not to say I don't respect other people's interests. You find politics fascinating?"

"No. I hate politics, actually." She felt an ounce of relief; it didn't last. His avoidance of newspapers explained why he hadn't recognized her, but Kip's face was still regularly plastered over the Missing Children's Network. Depending on when and how often he watched television...but she couldn't ask him that. Maybe she'd already seemed too curious.

"You haven't said how you like the Lakka."

"No?" She glanced down at her half-filled glass. It didn't taste like any liqueur she'd ever had before. The flavor was delicate and fruity, with a hint of sweetness that soothed her throat. "It's delicious," she admitted.

"It's made from cloudberries, I think I told you."

"Yes." He *had* to stop looking at her. He *had* to stop measuring every word as if he thought she were a terrified fawn that needed infinitely gentle handling to tame. She was no fawn. She was not "tamable." She was just a woman who was scared out of her mind.

"Sara?"

She looked up from the glass. In a dozen ways she'd picked up an invisible stream of steady messages that Jarl was safe, a good man, a man not likely to threaten or hurt her. It would be so tempting to delude herself.

Something was trying to happen between her and Jarl. Her heartbeat knew it. Her breasts were tight and hard. They knew it. Her skin felt permanently flushed and her pulse did a silly tap dance every time he looked at her. She couldn't let any of that happen.

"You're not so jumpy tonight," he mused quietly.

"Jumpy?" He had bold eyes, honest eyes. Too bold and too honest to make a lie of denial ring true.

"Jumpy," he repeated. "But then, maybe I'd have aimed a shotgun at a stranger if I'd been in your shoes—a woman alone on an island with a small boy. You still feel a little skittish, don't you? But you won't in time—not with me, not once you know me. And now—" he lurched to his feet, dusted the sand from his jeans, and flashed her a grin "—I have a sauna to plan with Kip."

Kip, so busy walking his turtle, sped back at the sound of his name.

"Wait a minute," she yelped. Her better instincts demanded that she put a halt to all this right now: the man, the way he looked at her, the way he was far too easily seeping into their lives.

And she would have, except for her son. The one with the prancing bare feet. The one with the hopeful blue eyes. The one with the impish grin. The one who—she couldn't believe it—had tucked his small hand into Jarl's.

"You can plan," she said weakly. "As long as you don't do anything about it. Kip, you can talk with Jarl about a sauna, but we're not going to do anything about it."

But the two of them planned until the sun set and a rising wind blew a blustering cluster of thunderclouds directly overhead. Jarl paced out a spot behind the porch. Kip paced out the same spot right after him. Jarl put his hands on his hips. Kip put his hands on his hips. Jarl tugged his ear. Kip tugged his ear. Jarl got out a measuring tape, and dead serious, Kip read off a "hundred zillion miles" as if those numbers existed on the tape.

"Now, we're talking about a *savu* sauna. The old fashioned kind," Jarl said.

"Hear that, Mom? We're talking about a sava sana."

"We *should* build it out of birch, but pine'll do if we can't find enough birch."

"Hear that, Mom? We need *birch*."

"We're going to need some special rocks."

"That's no problem. I'm great at finding rocks, Jarl. Nobody can find more rocks than me. Ask my mom."

"Is Kip very good at finding rocks, Sara?"

"Excellent," Sara affirmed, by then wondering why she bothered. Both included her in the conversation, but it was just token attention. She could have been sitting on the moon and neither of them would really have noticed.

Perched on the veranda steps, chin cupped in her hands, she watched the two with a smile she couldn't resist, a richness in her heart that kept building. Jarl wasn't faking the camaraderie with Kip. She had no idea if he had empathy with all children or just her son. She didn't care. It was the first inkling she had had that Kip was honestly going to be fine, that the scars he bore from Derek weren't permanent, that her son hadn't lumped all adult men in that one sad basket.

She mentioned bedtime twice. She was ignored.

She mentioned that it was getting far too dark for them to see. She was ignored.

She ignored a lot for quite a while, including her own good sense when she realized Jarl was serious about this *sava* sauna. She'd thought the idea was a whim, a lark. The way he talked to Kip, a sauna was a necessity to life, nothing one discussed or argued about, but was simply a given. Such a difference they had in cultural backgrounds!

This difference intrigued her. Curiosity tugged; questions bubbled in her mind. She found herself listening intently to the Finnish lore Jarl poured out lightly to Kip, wanting to hear more, wanting to hear the rich, deep drawl of Jarl's voice. Then she realized what she was doing. Here it was nine o'clock. The treetops were shaking like shaggy mops, and maybe the wind had chased away the mosquitoes but the temperature was dropping degrees by the minute. Sara stood up, put her hands on her hips, and adopted a general's sternness. "Enough."

"Ah, Mom."

"Jarl has to go home or he's going to get caught in a storm. And you have to go to bed, urchin. Right now."

"Mom—"

"Say good-night to Jarl and thank him for the turtle."

She plucked up her son and recited her thank-yous, too, for Kip's turtle, the dinner and the Lakka. Maybe it wasn't wise, but her verbal thank-yous were accompanied by eye contact. Warm, honest, real eye contact. It was the only way she knew how to express another kind of gratitude for the time he'd given her son.

She wrapped her son closer to her chest. He was heavy. "It takes me a while to get him tucked in," she hinted. The evening had been special. She didn't want to have to get rude again, didn't want to have to say that she wasn't inviting him inside or that he should leave now.

"I understand," he told her.

But he obviously didn't. She was nearly an hour getting Kip washed and tucked in and sung to, yet when she finally walked back out to the living room, he hadn't left. He was standing on her porch, his arms resting on the rail, looking out over the lake.

Nerves clustered in her stomach when she pushed open the screen door. The skies were rumbling, and the wind had picked up with a low, keening sound. Plummeting barometric pressure might have justified her sudden nervousness, but she knew that wasn't the true reason.

Jarl turned the moment she stepped outside, his features shadowed. His bare shoulders looked huge in the darkness, and his gaze fixed on her face. Until that moment, she'd almost convinced herself that befriending one small little boy was his only interest in the island.

"I didn't expect you to still be here. It's going to rain."

He nodded. "I'll be going, but I wanted to wait until I had the chance to ask you a question alone."

Alarm pulsed through her on a heartbeat pounding dread.

"It's about Kip, or I wouldn't be inclined to pry. The two of you are obviously alone on the island here, which means you could either be divorced or his father could be dead. Neither is my business, but there's no way I want to risk trampling on awkward or painful ground for the boy."

Her dread diminished. Of all the questions he could ask, this was one she could answer with relative honesty. "His father is alive, but there's no relationship." She added, "For Kip's sake, *please* don't bring up his father. If he brings up the subject, that's something else, but—"

"All right."

Actually, it wasn't. She heard her own words, and knew that her answer was the same as admitting she was willing for him to see Kip again. Kip... and her?

She averted her head, confused and exhausted at once. Too many physically long days, too much stress, too much to do, too much to worry about—she paid the heavy price for the choices she had made. It took a ceaseless, constant, concentrated effort to remind herself that she was a fugitive, that she had to think like a fugitive, that she could never be less than cautious and careful. Sometimes the whole thing crashed down. Sometimes she just couldn't be more than Sara. "Well..." She had to force the serious briskness in her tone.

He didn't budge.

She tried again. "I'm sure you have things you still want to do tonight."

"Actually, just one."

The man for whom her son had developed a blind, instinctive trust moved toward her. She guessed what he intended, but her brace of awareness had no hint of fear. There was no chance she could allow an embrace to happen. Fear didn't belong when a woman's choices were that clear.

Her choices might have been clear, but Jarl only moved closer. He didn't try to touch her, and that confused her. He simply stood there for a long time, a frown wedged on his forehead, his chest a stone wall blocking her view of the night. Even when his knuckles gently brushed her cheek, it didn't feel like a pass. And when his forefinger pushed a strand of hair from her forehead, she sensed nothing of aggression.

He smelled like sand and sea, and by the time he tilted her chin and placed his mouth on hers, he tasted like the cloudberry drink he'd brought for her to sample. *This is me, Sara. Just me. Now, weren't you silly to be so afraid of this?*

The wind dropped to a whisper. A kaleidoscope of color seemed to have gone mad in her head. She expected to *see* lightning in the sky, not to feel spears of it slash through her bloodstream. His lips were cool and smooth, slanted across hers with absorbing pressure. She had the quicksilver sensation that he was absorbing her, taking her in, draining her of willpower and sense.

Her hands latched onto his upper arm. His muscles contracted at her touch and he lifted his head. Dark eyes drifted over her face. He smiled, and then his second kiss began with that same smile, a kiss of lightness, softness, tenderness. The kiss changed the moment his tongue found hers.

She told herself to move. She reminded herself that the embrace was impossible and a relationship with any man out of the question. Any intimate, personal needs she had as a woman had been banished months ago. Kip came first, because he had to. For her son, she would never risk danger.

And Jarl kissed like danger, smelled like danger, tasted like danger. Yet not the danger that he would harm her. The terror was that her instincts, like her son's, told her to trust this man. Jarl had somehow won her son over by responding to a powerfully helpless need in the little one. But Lord, it had never once occurred to her that he could discover a very different kind of powerful need in her.

His thumb traced her collarbone, then slipped inside the neckline of her blouse. An awesome trembling enveloped her senses. This was not a physical trembling but an emotional one.

Sara lived every day in isolation, loneliness, fear. Every day she told herself she could handle that. And now, the slow sweep of his hands, the warm scent of his skin, the brush of silk-soft kisses wasn't threatening her. But being held somehow didn't feel good. It felt . . . hopelessly terrifying.

He leaned back, seeming to know there was a nice strong log wall to balance against. She only saw that it was dark. The wind was dark and wild. His thighs were rock-hard, anchoring her in a world turned blurred and vague. His strength and warmth and sureness were her ballast.

The knot of blouse at her midriff fell loose. Her heartbeat went singing, stinging fast when his callused palm claimed her breast. Air rushed into her lungs, expelled with nothing to replace it. How could a man's rough hand be so gentle? Her breasts swelled for his approval. Her nipples ached for the slow, tender rub of his thumb.

A hoarse, half-wild sound broke the silence. It must have come from her, because she heard him murmur something gruff and low and approving. He gathered her up, and the last of her good sense shattered.

She felt the thick, bristly texture of his hair under her fingertips, and knew her arms had gone around him. She felt the ache of muscles in her calves, and knew she'd willingly gone on tiptoe. His kisses no longer coaxed and wooed but took with elemental hunger, fierce desire, the passion of raw, wet heat. She knew, because she kissed him back in just that way. Each kiss was a match. She lit one. He lit one. Until every damn cell in her body was burning.

It was Jarl's fault. He was strong and real and lonely. His kisses were too wild, too fierce, not the kisses of a practiced lover but the embrace of a vulnerable man sharing that honesty. She realized now that he needed, too. He needed in a way that made her think of cold winter nights, spring-soft

whispers, summer heat, autumn color. He held her, and she
had the illusion of magic. He kissed her, and she believed.

The song in her blood had words: Stand by me, please,
please. I'm so damn scared. Maybe anything—maybe
everything—could be all right if he just held her and didn't
let go. A woman could always be strong when she had to be.
Sara was strong. But not always. No one could always be
strong. Just for a minute more. So badly, she needed someone strong enough to stand by her...

"Kissa, kissa."

The strange, foreign word whispered in her ears, a warn-
ing spoken hoarsely, a promise tendered in a fierce murmur. Shaken, she pulled back, and only then realized that
the pending storm had become real.

Rain drove into the shadowed veranda, not the first drops
of an opening storm, but the pelting drive of a fully developed downpour. Jarl's shoulders and back were soaked;
she'd felt nothing because his body had shielded her. But
nothing could shield her from the harsh intensity of passion she saw in his face, the possessive determination she
saw in his eyes.

"Yes," he said fiercely. "I think I knew the moment I
looked at you how it would be. So beautiful, Sara. Not easy,
not simple, but beautiful and dangerous and fragile. A
woman a man would guard from storms, dragons, all the
loneliness. Believe me. I'll be back."

His head was soaked the minute he stepped off the porch.
It took her seconds to understand he was leaving, really
leaving. It took a few more seconds for reality to slam,
crash, jam into her swimming head. Finally, the word burst
from her throat. "No!"

The wind picked up the desperation in that single sylla-
ble, hurled it toward him.

He turned once, his shoulders already gleaming wet, rain
streaming down his face in the darkness. "Tomorrow," he
told her.

"No!"

A slow, lazy smile showed his teeth. "Ah, *kissa*, you are terribly fond of that word. We'll have to teach you a bigger vocabulary. And we will. Starting tomorrow."

Four

By ten o'clock the next morning, ripped and broken shingles surrounded the old clubhouse in a miniwall. Boxes of new shingles were scattered all over the roof, and so were the contents of Jarl's tool box. His workboots were braced against the chimney, an open container of tar next to him,

Tar was an irreplaceable sealer. It was also a royal pain to work with. He had tar on his shoulder, the spatula, his hands, his chin, his boots, and even a little on the roof.

Last night's rain had washed the leaves and put a shine on the lake, but it hadn't diminished the heat wave. The morning sun was a baker. Even shirtless, sweat trickled down his spine and dampened the hair at the nape of his neck. A fly buzzed. He swatted it, and there was another tar smudge on his chest.

Methodically, he spread a spatula full of tar into place, reached for a shingle and then the hammer and nails. When he finished one patch, he moved to another. He was on the third when he heard the burst of laughter coming from the dockside of the woods.

He stopped working and waited. She hadn't seen him yet. The two of them were threading through the trees, Sara chasing Kip with a towel. Both of them were giggling, both dressed in nothing more than bathing suits. Sara's was a simple maillot, white, modest in cut. It was a serious swimmer's suit, and the kind that mercilessly showed off any flaws in a woman's figure.

Flaws, of course, were in the eye of the beholder. Jarl tried to critically judge the tight, tiny fanny, the nip of a waist, her button breasts. There was barely enough of her for a man to hold on to. She was so lithe, so slim. Her wet hair was plastered to her scalp. Her shoulders had a faint spray of freckles and, never mind the laughter, he could tell that she hadn't slept well. Her eyes had the violet smudge of exhaustion.

She was beautiful. His gaze dawdled again over her shoulders, eyes, hair, fanny. He claimed where his eyes touched, with an instinct as irrevocable and fierce as survival. Until last night he'd believed himself to be a reasonably civilized human adult male. Now he had a brilliant insight into the caveman mentality.

He was not letting her go. The skies could freeze, icebergs fry, the ground turn blue. Sara, though, was his.

A misplaced Finn of American citizenship who owned a simple hardware store in Pontiac, Michigan, was unused to such powerful thoughts. He was still bemused by the force of the draw he felt for this one small woman. Bemused, not confused. Shaken, but not unsure.

He knew she'd been married—she had a son—but it was hard for him to believe it. Last night her mouth had lain naked under his with an innocence and vulnerability that had unsteadied him. Last night she'd trembled in his arms like a woman just coming alive. Last night she'd totally destroyed the pride he had in himself as a lover. He thought he knew how to please a woman. He knew *nothing* of how to love Sara as she needed to be loved, as he wanted to love her, as he intended to love her.

He had spent a decade searching for a woman to match his passions, a woman strong and honest with emotion when it mattered, a woman loving enough to fight for. And the fight was on, he mused to himself, well aware the instant she spotted him. She stopped dead in the space of a second, and then, faster than a bullet, wrapped the towel around her and rushed toward him.

"Mr. Hendriks!"

They were back to Mr. Hendriks. And, poor baby, he saw the panic and anxiety clouding her eyes, the clutch hold she had on that towel. One of these days he was going to hold her down until she told him exactly what she was so terrified of, but not at this moment when she was trying so hard to look prancing mad. "Good morning," he called down amiably.

"Hi, Jarl!"

One of two, at least, was delighted to see him. "Hi, squirt."

"What are you doing up there?" Sara persisted.

"It rained last night," he said reasonably. "When I looked at your roof yesterday, I figured you must have four leaks, maybe five. What you really need is a new roof, but a decent patch job will get you through another season. I know the new shingles look strange now, but they're of a color with the old ones; once they weather a little they'll blend in." Possibly she lacked interest in the little details, because she interrupted him with a voice like a slice.

"That's not the point."

"No?" He nodded. "Well, I'd rather tackle the sauna before the roof—the sauna won't take any time at all—but I was pretty sure the roof would be your first priority." To the little one, he murmured sotto voce, "No higher than the first two rungs, Kip. We don't want to make your mommy nervous."

"I am not nervous. And you will immediately get down from there!"

"If you insist that I tackle the sauna first—"

"You are not tackling any sauna!"

"So we agree. My first priority is the roof."

Not that he could read her mind, but he had a feeling she was very close to shaking the ladder. Instead, she abruptly ducked her head, kissed her son, and sent him into the house with bribes of a cookie and orders to dress. When that was done, she heaved a sigh loud and exasperated enough to puff up her chest and climbed the ladder rungs until she reached the eaves.

He set his hammer down and adopted an appropriately serious expression to match the terrible gravity of her own. "This has gone on far enough, Jarl. You and I are going to have a talk," she said firmly.

"Good idea." He locked his arms across his chest, a good listening posture.

"You certainly don't do this to other people. Walk around finding strangers' docks to fix, strangers' roofs to patch."

"Never once," he agreed.

"You can't just..." She motioned vaguely with her hands.

He understood the motion. "I can't," he agreed.

Color rushed to her cheeks, more than the blush of the sun justified. "And as for last night, I..." She swallowed, and for a moment seemed to lose her voice altogether. Whispers should be so fragile. Her eyes had the shadow of softness, the plea of longing, the defeat of fibs that had to be told. Jarl had the sudden disquieting insight that if he ever found the man who'd hurt her he would be capable of tearing another human being limb from limb. "Jarl," she began helplessly.

"I'm listening."

"Look, last night was wrong. Something I didn't want to happen. I don't know why it did, but it doesn't matter. I'm not looking for a man. I'm not looking for a man or a lover or a friend. I don't know how to make it plainer than that."

"You've made your feelings very plain," he encouraged her.

"I want to be left alone."

He nodded. "Is that about all you want to say?"

"Yes!"

"Fine. I'll be in for lunch. And while you're busy making lunch, I want you to make a long list of all the other things that have been bothering you. I believe a man and woman should air all their problems, talk out these things. Next time, don't hold so much back. How am I going to know where I stand if you're going to continue to be so shy?"

Silence. Her lips twisted up in a fascinating way. He guessed she was considering murdering him. She was also— certainly unwillingly—beginning to laugh.

"Jarl."

"Yes, *kissa*?"

If she didn't understand the endearment, she must have understood the tone. Peach streaked her cheeks. Her eyes turned a hopeless, helpless sapphire. "You are driving me bananas."

"Ah." He shook his head, a consoling gesture.

"You don't listen."

"I listen very carefully. What I never do is argue," he corrected her.

She closed her eyes for one long second. "Is there something I am failing to say to make you stay away from here?" she asked almost humorously.

"Not a thing."

"You're really not going to go away, are you?"

So weary, so angry, so exasperated. And spikes of hair were drying around her cheeks; it looked very silly where she had dragged a hand through it. Her nose had a dot of sunburn. Her nipples were hard little nubs, straining against the wet suit. Maybe the maillot was modest, but he hoped no other man had seen her in it.

He said softly, very softly, "There is no chance of my leaving you alone. I knew that the day I met you. You knew that last night, so resign yourself. And for now, scoot. I have work to do."

"Can I put the raisins on, Mom?"

"Sure, punkin." Each sandwich had been cut in four

parts. She watched Kip pop two raisins for eyes into each section.

"Marshmallows?"

"Coming up." One tiny marshmallow made a nose in each small square.

"Carrots!"

"Carrots!" Sara echoed her son, and produced carrot curls for the smile. If Mr. Hendriks didn't care for face sandwiches and peanut butter celery boats for lunch, he had a problem. She made lunch for Kip, not for overbearing Finns who walked around half-naked and kissed like sin.

"Can I go get him now?"

"First, ask Jarl if he wants water or milk. Tell him that's all we have."

Mr. Hendriks wanted milk. Sara wanted him to go home. The kitchen had originally been constructed to feed twenty Boy Scouts, but he made it seem small the minute he walked in. In one quick glance he took in her red checked curtains, the fresh paint, her charcoal sketches of doves and gulls.

He took the chair by Kip instead of at the head of the table where she'd set his glass. She switched his milk for her water, swished napkins on the table, then sat down. Why she sat down was a good question. There was no possibility she had any appetite.

He smelled like solvent and soap and had thrown on a sweatshirt. The solvent had missed two patches of tar on his arm; his sweatshirt was a rag. He looked brawny, tough and happy. He was probably very satisfied with himself; it was the first time she'd let him in past the screen door.

"It looks delicious, Sara."

"Thank you." She braced herself for a comment about raisins-and-carrot-curl faces; it didn't happen. When Jarl chugged milk, Kip chugged milk. When Jarl bit into a sandwich, Kip did, too. Her son, always a fussy eater, devoured six of the little squares before he was through, which was ample justification for his mother's stunned silence.

Her silence, though, had no relationship to shock. She was thinking hard and desperately. And instead of thinking from her point of view, she was trying very hard to think from his. Jarl saw a lonely little boy. A shaggy, half-tamed island that needed repairs and man-type labor everywhere you turned. A single mother coping alone, who, perhaps, he happened to feel a little attraction for.

"You two take a long swim every morning?" Jarl asked her.

"Always. Kip's been a swimmer since he was six months old."

"I give Mom lessons every morning," Kip started to explain, and then yelped, "Whoops!"

"It's okay, punkin." Sara flew up for a rag. A meal without a spill would have been like rain without water. One didn't fuss over the inevitable. She mopped his arm, the chair, the floor, then sat down again. She picked up a piece of stuffed celery, but instead of eating it, held it like a buoy on a hurricane-swept ocean.

She had only one priority: protecting her son. Any chance of public exposure and discovery was a risk to Kip.

How to protect him, though, wasn't proving to be a simple set of choices where Jarl was concerned. Jarl knew Kip liked him. He knew she needed help. He knew—darn her perfectly insane response the night before—that she was not immune to him. If she protested his presence too forcefully, wouldn't it be likely to arouse his suspicion and curiosity? Wasn't it really safer for her son, for her, to play the role he'd assigned her: that of a woman simply a little over-wary because she was alone.

There were no safe choices, not from the moment Jarl had set foot on the island. A barbed-wire ball twisted in her stomach. There had been no safe choices for her from long before that.

"Kip?" Jarl dusted the crumbs from his hands onto the plate, and leaned forward, elbows on the table. "You and I have a big job to do this afternoon."

"I'm ready," Kip informed him passionately.

"Actually, we have several jobs." Jarl directed his attention solely toward the child, as if he didn't notice Sara. All during lunch he hadn't missed her silence, scarce appetite or the fragile look of strain in her eyes. He figured he could have solved a lot of problems if he'd snatched her on his lap and kissed her silly, but there was Kip. Kissing Kip's mother the way Kip's mother badly needed kissing was not for a four-year-old's eyes. "I figure it's going to take me about a half hour to finish the roof. That I have to do alone, and sometime over the afternoon you and I have to spend a couple hours on the sauna. That's a must."

"I know," Kip agreed.

"But we have another, even more important job."

"I know," Kip repeated with certainty, and then propped his chin in his hands. "What job?"

"We have to make your mother laugh." Sara blinked, glancing up. Jarl paid no attention.

"My mom?"

"Yup."

Kip scrunched his nose. "That's not a job. That's easy. Mom laughs all the time." He thought. "I know some special tricks, though."

"Such as?" Jarl prompted him.

"You can do somersaults. Whenever I do somersaults, she laughs. Or you can play blocks or color with her. She always laughs when we're playing blocks." Kip sneaked him a look. "You're probably too big to play blocks."

"Nope. I like blocks."

"Don't bring her any bugs. She does not laugh when you bring her bugs." His face lit up. "But you can blow on her tummy. Nobody laughs like Mom when you blow on her tummy. You should see her—"

"KIP!"

"Ticklish, is she?"

"Nobody, but nobody, is ticklish like my—"

"Boys, you are banished from this kitchen," Sara announced firmly.

"That means we have to get out of here," Kip informed Jarl. "The plate goes in the trash, the glass goes on the counter. You don't want to get yelled at."

"I sure don't."

"She doesn't really yell much. She just says she's going to, but I'll tell you this. You gotta remember to flush."

"I'll try."

His expression was so deadpan that Sara had the hopeless inclination to laugh, but the two didn't give her time. Kip tossed his plate in the trash. Jarl did the same. Kip pushed his glass on the counter; Jarl set his next to it. On days she couldn't coax her son into a nap, part of the post-lunch ritual was for her to stand at the door, bend down and give Kip a quick smack before he sprang outside. She did that, but on the upswing to a straight position, Jarl was waiting for her at a grown-up height, as if to say "my turn."

So fast, too fast, the devil laid a kiss on her mouth that had her senses scattering. The kiss was sassy. Disrespectful. A tease of tongues and a nibble on her upper lip, and at the same time his palm cupped her bottom and squeezed.

She was appalled. Even more appalled when he lifted his head and studied her flushed face with a self-satisfied grin. "You look wonderful just kissed," he told her, "but you'll look even better just loved." He put his hand on the door. "You've got a long afternoon ahead of you, woman."

She knew, but later, knew she hadn't exactly realized how long it would be. The Finn thought he could sing. Her son couldn't, and the blend of baritone and squeaky soprano through the long afternoon nearly drove her out of her mind.

The two of them did work. They piled and torched the dead shingles, then Jarl produced a saw from his boat. The two felled a tall, thin pine—the most exciting thing Kip had ever seen. While Jarl sawed the long trunk into measured lengths, Kip had the job of collecting the biggest lake stones he could find.

About the time she realized he was actually determined to build this crazy sauna, she was caught. She needed a sauna about as much as she needed a burst appendix. She needed a man complicating her entire life like she needed a herd of buffalo, but her son... Watching Kip prancing and animated and so innocently joyful was addictive.

I'm going to have to get tough with Jarl, she kept telling herself, but by then Jarl and Kip had descended on her like two marshaling generals. She was given a shovel and told to dig. What for, she had no idea. The lake stones and logs and the hole they were digging all obviously related to his sauna-building, but she still doubted the results. As far as she could tell, all they were accomplishing was a huge, terrible, filthy mess, and their incessant singing would drive a teetotaler to drink.

Her shoveling failed to please them, and she was banished to a supervisory role at the top of the knoll. She had sumac to chop, weeds to kill, an ankle-high yard to clear, a kitchen to clean. Every time she tried to sneak off, she got a roaring, "Stay there and get some sun, woman!"

And then Kip's mimicking soprano, "Stay there and get some sun, woman!" Immediately followed by, "Why are we calling her woman, Jarl? Her name is Mom. Didn't you know?"

She kept telling herself that any sane woman in her shoes would be having a heart attack. The bond her son was forming with this man couldn't be allowed. Memories of her dissolving in his arms the night before should never have happened. And when she recalled Jarl's intimate sass in the kitchen at lunch, she wondered how she had ever allowed things to get so out of hand.

But so much conspired against her common sense. The sun was shining. Summer heat was its own lethargy-inducing drug, and the island was a rain-washed Eden. For so long, so terribly long, she'd been afraid Derek had scarred Kip so badly that he'd never trust another man, and her son was opening up right in front of her eyes. And as for Jarl...

Watching Jarl was like watching a disaster happening. He'd started out a decent-looking man and was gradually transforming into a muddy reject. Long before the digging project was completed, she'd lost her son under piles of sand and sawdust. Jarl and Kip were becoming two of a kind. Their skin color was sweat-streaked dirt, and two pairs of navy jeans had spatters and blotches of everything from wet dirt to pine dust.

By four in the afternoon, the disgraceful pair climbed her knoll and looked down at her with a matching set of masculine hands on hips. "Sad," Jarl said disgustedly.

"Very sad," Kip agreed, and then whispered, "What's sad?"

"Look at your mother. A disgrace. Filth from her head to her toes, fingernails a mess, can't even see her face...." He shook his head. "What are we going to do with her, Kip?"

"I don't know. What are we going to do with her?" Kip was dancing in anticipation.

Sara drawled, "I hate to tell you this, boys, but I'm the clean one. It's you two—"

"Sass from the peanut gallery!" Jarl roared.

"What are we going to do with her?" Kip roared, soprano style.

"Your mother desperately needs a bath."

"No."

"A little dunk in the lake."

"NO!"

"Clothes and all!"

"Don't you dare. Don't you dare! I'll—"

"Kip, grab a bar of soap from the house. We're going to get your mother clean. This is disgraceful!"

"Omigosh! Omigosh!"

Her son had never seen anything so funny as his mom being carted over a man's shoulder. He thought her chortled yelp even funnier in that bare instant before Jarl tossed her in the icy lake. The best for Kip, though, was when Jarl tugged a sopping Sara to her feet and started lathering her shirt and jeans.

Sara tried to tell herself that she was mad. She was certainly wet, she was definitely cold, and horseplay between a woman and a man raised veiled memories of her ex-husband. It brought out fears of violence, nightmares of a man physically stronger than she was. And maybe that was exactly why she felt her rigid and impenetrable moorings ripping loose.

Jarl wasn't Derek. He was nothing like Derek. He was standing in waist-deep water with his wet hair flopped on his forehead and dirt and water streaks flowing down his face. He was singing like Sinatra. He was sudsing the sleeves of her shirt with her in it. Kip was laughing so hard he was holding his stomach...and suddenly she was laughing, too. Not a little laugh, but the big, silly, joyful, tummy-shaking kind.

"That's it! I'm going to get you for this—both of you!—you think I won't? Your lives aren't worth marshmallows. When I get my hands on you two—and where's that soap? Now you're in trouble!"

They both splashed away from her with their spines curved like Cs, yelling like banshees as she chased after them. There was just an instant before she caught them. An instant when Jarl suddenly turned. An instant when the sky blazed bluer, when the sun burned stronger, when her heart felt as fluff-light as the clouds.

It was just a moment lost in time, so short it couldn't be measured. All he did was look at her. He wasn't laughing any less hard but there was something more, a glimmer of something protective and fiercely intimate in his brown eyes.

Her laughter mattered to him.

A soft, slow fire seeped through her bloodstream. Control had to dominate her life. She had no room for carefree play, for innocence. Celibacy was one of the prices she'd paid for the choices she'd made. She was not supposed to feel need any more. She couldn't share, she couldn't trust, she couldn't want. She'd stopped believing in happiness for herself—not just seven months but years ago.

It all suddenly snapped, like a rubber band stretched too tight. The look in Jarl's eyes was as dangerous as softness, as sweet as yearning, as sexy as a silvery, shimmering awareness of the way a man and woman could be together.

She wanted that look. She needed it. She *had* to believe there was someone there, someone she could trust. She *had* to believe that one quick-quick moment of happiness wasn't wrong. From the heart, from the soul, she needed to believe that he wouldn't hurt her.

"Sara." Jarl's hand stretched out to her.

The ice-cold water danced under the sun. Summer heat drugged the air she took into her lungs. No sky, ever, had been this blue. Her son's laughter caught on the sleek hot breeze, and she felt the pulse of her heart, beating lonely and scared and so damned hard, under her sopping shirt.

She took Jarl's hand, probably because she was totally insane.

For that moment . . . for just that moment . . . she didn't care.

Five

———

We don't have to work on anything today, do we?"

"Nope, it's a play day." Jarl, intent on threading fishing wire through the pole, didn't look up.

"So we're gonna fish all morning. And before dinner, you and me are gonna take our first sauna."

"Right."

"And even though a sauna's a bath, we don't have to use any soap. No matter what Mom says."

"Hmmm." When Jarl set the poles in the boat, he sneaked Sara a wink. She was sitting cross-legged on the dock, less than two feet from her son. Kip seemed to have the interesting misconception that when he was talking to one adult the other was conveniently deaf.

Kip had one foot balanced on the other and his arms burrowed under his sweatshirt. He couldn't stand still. Even the freckles on his nose were in motion. "I'm going as fast as I can. Two more minutes and we'll be ready, short stuff," Jarl promised him.

"And Mom doesn't get to go. It's just you and me."

"Just you and me," Jarl echoed, possibly for the thirty-seventh time.

"No girls allowed. Not on fishing trips."

"Actually girls are allowed on fishing trips."

"But not this time. Not for trout."

Actually, girls were also allowed on trout-fishing expeditions, but taking Kip out alone this once was Jarl's goal. A week ago Sara was as inseparable from her son as peanut butter and jelly. Even now she wasn't easy about it, but she was letting it happen. He figured he'd cajoled her into a state of sheer exhaustion. But Sara didn't wear down easily.

After lifting the tackle box into the boat, Jarl reached for the life preservers. Early morning sun glazed the lake. Leaves ruffled in a bare breeze, and the sky was golden. Sara's delicate, sculpted features were washed in sunlight and her lips curved in a smile.

She was so precious that sometimes he didn't know what to do with the huge, thick feeling she caused in his throat.

He kept telling himself that he couldn't be in love with her this soon. Talk didn't help and "this soon" was relative. He'd sneaked hours on hours with her this last week. When Sara forgot her defenses, a warm and passionate woman came out of hiding, a woman who drank in the smallest offerings of laughter and kindness. She listened. She could be almost annoyingly perceptive of his feelings.

She was also strong and stubborn. Too strong. Too stubborn. She'd quit fighting his right to be in her life only after she'd established the rules of the relationship. Hot, lazy days and a shimmering sun, honeysuckle smells and desultory conversations and flirtations were the flavors of summer. Vacationers made casual, temporary, summer friendships, then passed out of each other's lives. That's what she wanted.

It was also the only way she was willing to play. He'd gone along. He'd carefully not asked her why she never left the island. Where she came from, where she was going or what the hell she was so scared of.

If frustration was slowly driving him out of his mind, he didn't let it show. The Finnish language had no future tense. A Finn had no way to say, "You *will* trust me." A Finn said, "You *are* trusting me."

He'd been proving that premise, whether or not Sara was aware of it. She'd stopped trying to discourage him when he joined their daily swim. She was starting to forget herself and set a place for him at dinner. Her protests had been ferocious but short when he'd tackled scraping and painting her windows. And his Lakka had found a place in her cupboard.

The real measure of her trust, though, was that so-reluctant permission given for her three-foot-two-inch sidekick to fish with him—the one with the shaggy caramel bangs and antsy feet. "Ready?"

"You bet!" Permission given, he scrambled into the boat and beamed at Sara. "I'm leaving you, Mom! And you don't get to go!"

"I know that, lovebug. And I hope you catch a fish."

"Just me and Jarl are going."

"No kidding?"

"We may let you go next time, but I'll have to ask Jarl. This is strictly boy stuff."

"Ah, well."

"We're going now. Bye!"

She stood up to wave them off, her big shirt flapping around her hips, her hair blowing in the bare breeze. Suddenly her demeanor changed. He knew the exact instant she completely changed her mind about the whole expedition. Her glow suddenly paled. Her smile turned artificial. Her arms wrapped around her body as if she were protecting herself from arctic winds, and her gaze pinned his across the water. Take care of my son, she seemed to say.

Sara chided herself for such foolishness. Jarl loved the pint-sized devil, which she knew well. He'd lose both arms before he let anything happen to Kip.

The lake was spring-fed. As soon as they reached a cold spot, Jarl dropped anchor and angled down so Kip was straddled between his legs. "We ready?"

"Gosh, yes."

Kip liked the worms. He liked casting even more. Jarl figured the urchin's chances of catching a trout were about a million to one. Kip cast with a four-year-old's violent exuberance that must have scared every fish as far as the next lake, but by then Jarl had his own pole in the water. He figured he could substitute poles if and when he got a bite.

That was the plan. The plan went to holy hell after five minutes. From nowhere Kip's smile drooped and his lower lip puckered.

"We have to go back," he told Jarl.

"You can't be tired of fishing already?"

"No."

There was nothing else, just those big eyes turned sad. "Hey." Jarl slipped both poles in holders so he had hands free to swaddle the little one's shoulders. "We got a problem here I don't know about? I was pretty sure you wanted to go fishing."

"I do."

"Well then?"

So grave, so soft, his head tilted back to face Jarl. "I forgot. I don't leave my mom."

Jarl hesitated, and then said gently, "I really think she'll be okay on the island—for just a few minutes—without you."

"No, she won't. She'll say she's okay, but she won't be. She'll be scared. I have to go back."

Jarl took another look at the boy's face, swore mentally and promptly pulled the poles out of the water. He wanted to say something, but didn't know what. More than that he wanted to do something. Smashing a brick wall would do.

Hadn't he been patient? But enough was enough. A four-year-old took fear for granted. It was time to put a stop to it. The little boy's mother was all through handling her mysterious, private nightmare alone. "Kip?"

"Can't you hurry?"

He was already paddling faster than the speed of sound. Dammit, *was* she sitting on that island alone and afraid? Low, quiet, he said, "Just so you know. I'm taking you back because you asked me to, but not because there's anything to be afraid of. I wouldn't let anything or anyone hurt you or your mother. There's nothing to be scared of."

"Yes, there is."

"Tell me."

But the tyke turned mute. Rapunzel had her tower. Kip and Sara had matching protective shells they climbed into whenever he came too close. An honorable man wouldn't have baited a child for information. Jarl would have bribed, cajoled, and begged Kip if he thought doing so would bring him answers, but Kip wouldn't talk.

His shoulders were tense by the time they reached shore. Kip's broodiness disappeared, though, the instant he spotted Sara at a distance down the beach. Sara turned at his yell. The two met in a bear hug, but by the time Jarl reached her, her eyes were questioning.

"We changed our minds, decided we had too much we wanted to do around the island instead," Jarl said easily.

"But I thought you both wanted to—"

"It's fine, Sara. Everything's fine." Or, Jarl thought, it would be.

Sara barely saw the two until they'd christened their first sauna and came in to dinner. Both scarfed down food like starving wolves. Kip couldn't stop talking about the sauna and about eggs. Mostly about eggs. "See, Mom, this whole world was an egg once upon a time. Half the yellow part turned into the sun. Half the white part turned into the moon. And guess what happened to the rest of the egg?"

"It got scrambled?" Sara guessed.

"No, silly. It got put in two parts, too. Half's heaven and half's us. You get me?"

"I get you."

Jarl murmured, "I just want you to know this is a brand-new version of the folktale."

"Did the story get a little transformed in the retelling?"

"A bit."

"What's *transformed*?" Kip demanded.

"*Transformed* means you get a brownie for dessert if you eat all your peas. Did Jarl tell you any other Finnish stories?"

"Sure. You tell her about the spirits, Jarl," Kip insisted and then rushed in, "See, if you want something from a tree, all you do is ask it nice. Because trees have spirits. So does water, so you can ask water for stuff, too. But you have to do it nice. You have to do it with manners. Like this." Kip swooped his fallen napkin from the floor, stuffed it in the front of his shirt, and pointed to it. "See? This is manners."

"Terrific," Sara said. "But now show me peas. On the spoon, urchin."

"Ah, Mom."

That night, for the first time in forever, Kip didn't protest going to bed, didn't freeze when she tried to leave the room.

She climbed back downstairs in a bemused mood. Bemused, beguiled, bewitched? This last week all three had kept close company, but never more than tonight. Jarl was sprawled in a chair, looking like only a man. Not an urchin charmer. Not a magician who waved a wand to make her life easier. Not like a Scandinavian devil who could woo lazy, easy laughter from a woman who had absolutely nothing to laugh about.

He'd lit a kerosene lantern. Its light glowed on the log walls and cavernous six-foot stone fireplace. Fireflies winked just outside the screen door.

He patted the seat next to him, knowing, as she did, that she wouldn't take it. Right after Kip went to bed, there were always blocks and crayons and Matchbox cars to scoop up and put away. She started scooping. "I owe you diamonds, rubies, whatever you want," she told him.

His eyes glinted with dark amusement. "What did I do?"

"You know what you did. He went to sleep in a snap. He's been bubbling happy all day, and all because of the time you spent with him. You this good with other little ones, or is it just mine?"

"I'm partial to yours."

"I am, too, but I'm also aware he can outchatter a magpie and wear out an Eveready battery." When the toys were put away, she pushed off her shoes and grinned. "I owe you. So what's it going to be? Emeralds? Brownies? Your own harem direct from the Middle East? Name it."

He chuckled. "Mom didn't appreciate a little break this afternoon, did she?"

"Mom got so much work done this afternoon she doesn't know what to do with herself. So what do you want for your reward?"

"If you're serious...." Jarl drawled.

"I am. As long as you don't pick the harem or the emeralds."

He chuckled again, but his eyes rested on her face with a sudden intimate intensity. He had a way of looking at her that made warmth pool in her stomach and reminded her of wild, drugging kisses in the rain. Those feminine pricklings were her cue to back off, stop teasing, be careful of waking sleeping bears.

Tonight she didn't take the cue. Maybe she'd faced fear so long that recklessness was becoming an old friend. A week ago the game had been something in her head. The game stated that she was safe with Jarl, that she could trust him, that there was nothing so dangerous about those rare, stolen moments of happiness.

Only it didn't seem like a game anymore. What Jarl had done and continued to do for her son was real. She was physically, mentally, and emotionally incapable of driving away a man who was that good for her little boy. And if she wanted to be honest, her Finn with the sexy, dark eyes and quiet, stubborn ways meant even more to her than he did to Kip.

She needed him. She wanted him. Until he'd barged into her life, she hadn't felt alive as a woman in years. You're in way, way over your head, Sara Chapman, she reminded herself.

But the velvet noose around her neck kept tightening. Yes, she could have found some way to chase him away, if it hadn't been for her son, if she hadn't been afraid of arousing his suspicion and curiosity. Allowing a casual friendship had seemed her safest choice. His vacation had a finite time span. Wasn't her safest choice still to keep the relationship carefully light, breezy, no questions, simple?

Safe for Kip.

As for herself, she felt as safe as a woman balancing on a tightrope in a high wind. But tonight nothing was that complicated. She curled a fist on her hip. "You'd better make up your mind pretty quick about that second brownie. The offer to wait on you hand and foot only lasts for another thirty-three seconds."

"Pity." Jarl eased off the sofa and stretched, lazy as a lion, his skin a cinnamon-bronze by lamplight. "Actually, I'll forgo the brownie and collect a different reward. In fact, payment for a free afternoon for Mom was set this morning at around eight o'clock."

"Eight o'clock?"

"When I started the fire in the sauna. You didn't think I built the thing just for Kip, did you? The fire's still hot and waiting. But first things first. Let's see all this monumental work you did this afternoon."

Her afternoon's illustrations were drying on the mantel. Grave as an art critic, he examined each one, while Sara trailed after him with an oddly clicking heartbeat.

She'd easily and readily shared her work with Jarl for a week now. Why not? It was one of few areas in which she could be totally honest with him. His judgment of her work wasn't what caused her clicking heartbeat, though; the sauna did.

She'd let him build the thing for one reason and one reason only. It mattered to Kip. She'd have let Jarl build a

thousand saunas if it would have quickened and insured the
emotional healing her son desperately needed. There was an
area, though, where she could not help her son, where only
a man could make the real difference in Kip's life. Jarl,
whether he'd meant to or not, had made that difference.
She'd deliberately and totally avoided the sauna project and
had planned on keeping it that way.

"Special, every picture," Jarl said finally.

"You're hopelessly biased. I've done better." She added
swiftly, "I didn't realize how late it was . . ."

"Barely nine."

"Both of us have had a long day."

"Sara."

"Yes?"

When had he moved so close? His eyes were as black as
ebony and his smile was disarmingly gentle. The night oozed
with intimacy. Jarl looked dark and muscular and inti-
mately male. His thumb brushed her cheek. "Saunas aren't
about sex," he said quietly.

"For heaven's sake. I never thought—"

He really smiled then. "*Kissa*, I would love to seduce you.
You've made it very clear that you're only in the market for
a noncomplicated friend. That's not how I feel about you.
Which you know. That's not how you feel about me. Which
you also know."

"Jarl—"

"We'll postpone all that for another time. Saunas have to
do with nakedness, but they have nothing to do with sex. A
male rabbit would wilt in that kind of heat and humidity,
you understand? We're talking about relaxing and about
something I want to share with you. Nothing more."

Images of wilting rabbits trounced her ability to concen-
trate. "Look, you sassy Finn . . ."

But she already knew she was giving in. Maybe heat and
sweat weren't her cup of tea, but he obviously thought his
sauna was the sun and the moon. It mattered to him. Lord
knew she owed him. So if her heart was drumming warn-
ings about being naked with Jarl, she forced it to stop. She'd

trusted him with her son, hadn't she? And he hadn't once pushed any kind of intimacy with her this past week. If he wanted her to take his ridiculous sauna, she would go.

She changed her mind twenty minutes later—the exact moment when she stepped barefoot off the veranda onto the ice-cold grass on a very black night wearing a scant towel and a scowl.

By the time she pushed open the sauna's small door, she was shivering, nervous, and smart with hindsight. She didn't want to do this. Caves gave her claustrophobia, and his little domed structure was as tiny and dark as a dungeon. The only light came from the corner, where a bed of lake stones framed a glow of coals. One pine bench stretched the length at ground level, with another just above it. Those were the only furnishings beyond a pail of cold water and some leafy branches collected for God knows what reason. The smoke was eye-smarting and the distinctive smell of hot, wet pine nostril-pinching strong. The temperature was about a million degrees, and that was Fahrenheit.

"This is fun, hmm?"

"Now, *kissa*. Don't get sassy until you've given it a try."

His mysterious endearment always made her too nervous to ask him what the word meant. Once her eyes had adjusted to the darkness, she discovered new cause for unease. Crouched on the ground, Jarl was cupping cold water on the coals, causing—and who needed it?—mountains more steam. Shadow and light roamed his angular thighs and spine. Flesh and muscle moved with mobile suppleness. If he'd worn a loincloth he would have had the look of a powerful, primitive caveman. Only he didn't have a loincloth.

She jerked her eyes away from him, and completely missed his grin when he gently snatched the towel away from her.

"You don't take a bath with a towel on, do you?"

"On Tuesdays I do."

He chuckled. "You take the bottom bench the first time. It's hotter on top."

"It couldn't be," she said dryly. Her hair was doomed to turn into an Afro, she couldn't breathe for the humidity, and Mr. Hendriks was so unself-conscious of his nude body that you'd think he was walking around in a tux. She gingerly sat down on the humid, damp bench and wondered vaguely what to cover up first.

"Lie down," Jarl ordered her.

When cats flew.

"Lie down," he repeated, much more softly.

Lord, he was stubborn. She flipped onto her stomach, a position that at least covered the most intimate body parts. He climbed over her to reach the top bench. Seconds passed. By the time she risked a look, it seemed all her blood pressure problems were for nothing. Lying on his back on the bench above her, his eyes were closed, his body totally relaxed.

She had no intention of relaxing. The cloying steam and close quarters had her heart pumping too hard. She wondered how long one had to suffer in these things. It was amazing, what some people thought was fun.

But when Jarl didn't move or talk, she didn't, either, and over time a sneaky languor invaded her consciousness. She had to breathe slowly and deeply or she couldn't breathe at all. Gradually her limbs and skin grew heavy, limp, lethargic, and a euphoric laziness stole into her pores.

Darkness and heat, darkness and heat, the hiss of water spitting on steam. Her whole body glazed with moisture, and she lost all sense of time. She couldn't think. This wasn't real. Reality was the Chapmans and Derek and feeling hunted. It was constant worry and no-choice anxiety, fear, helplessness, hopelessness, answers that didn't exist.

This was another world, a soft, soothing womb of darkness, a heat, a peace that seeped into her soul. There was no question of fighting it. She'd lost the energy and power to blink. Ever moving again was out of the question.

Silently, Jarl turned on his side to look down at her. In the glow of coals, shadows played on the curves and slopes of her backside. The hollow of her spine was a pocket of darkness. Her fanny glowed pearl-creamy. She glistened. Her cheek was resting on an arm; her lips curved in a half smile. He wondered if she could ever, would ever, look half so vulnerable again.

"Relaxed?"

"Marshmallows can't talk," she murmured back regretfully. Through thick, heavy lashes she saw his face above her, his eyes black as wet stones, fierce and dark and possessive by firelight. A trick of the darkness? Her breath caught and then expelled. It was only Jarl. "I'm not leaving," she told him. "You got me in here, so it's your fault. I'm just telling you now. I'm never leaving."

He smiled. "Relaxing is Part One of a sauna. Now we have to move to Part Two."

"Moving is not possible."

"It will be. Trust me."

When he stepped down, his body blocked the view of the coals. From the collection of small branches near the fire, he chose one, dipped it in the pail of water and swished it over the coals. Steam swirled in clouds of radiant heat. He did it again, and again, and then turned to her with the switch in his hand.

"Sit up for me," he murmured, his tone distracted, intense, serious.

"Umm . . . Jarl . . ."

Maybe he heard the quicksilver catch in her voice. "Don't get your hopes up, *kissa*. I'm not into S&M." His whisper had a tease of humor, but also a tease of a hidden scold. "The little switch is called a *vihta*, and using it is a very old custom that most have forgotten. It won't hurt you. I would never hurt you, which you know. And it will make you feel wonderfully good and alive. Sit up. Close your eyes."

Irritably, it occurred to Sara that he assumed, far too easily, that she trusted him. He assumed bareness and vulnerability were natural dynamics between them. He assumed she would simply believe any darn thing he told her.

"Kissa?"

She sat up and closed her eyes, feeling sleepy, fragile, lost. She did trust him. To a degree that should have warned her of what deep water she'd waded into. Instead, she felt immersed in the freedom and luxury of feeling safe, protected, snared in a dark, silken web that only this man could spin.

Lightly, swiftly, softly he plied his birch *vihta* on her thighs, her back, her throat and arms, her belly. Her skin was wet and the little lash caused a tingling prickle. There was no pain, only a sensation of sensual stimulation so intense that her first reaction was embarrassment, self-consciousness. Had she seriously gone crazy? A man was standing over her with a branch. How could she possibly feel good?

But he didn't hurt her. His *vihta* ritual had nothing to do with pain and everything to do with pleasure. Her skin woke up and glowed under the light beats, the soft lashes. She had the shimmering awareness that Jarl was as absorbed in her reactions as she was, that a line was being crossed and a bond being forged that was more intimate than sex. She felt naked from the inside out and he knew it. She felt whole and clean and come-alive feminine and so damn good. He knew.

"You like?" he whispered.

It was like asking a woman if she liked to climax. Mute, hopelessly limp, she simply looked at him. He smiled, and then turned.

"For Part Three of your sauna we need a little heat."

This time, he dribbled half the pail over the coals, and the heat and humidity exploded like dynamite.

"Jarl—"

"Two more minutes."

In two more minutes she was close to broiling. The sensation of contentment and well-being was no less overwhelming, but nearly more than she could handle.

"The lake now, Sara."

Her eyes blinked open. "You have to be joking?"

"You won't believe how good the cold water will feel."

"How about if you go and I just believe you?"

He chuckled, grabbed the towels and reached out for her hand.

"I can't. Trust me, I know what I'm talking about. I don't even have the energy to lift a small toe."

After all this time she should know that arguing with the Finn was useless. He bullied her out, slow, coaxing, like he'd tease someone out of a dream. It was still half a dream when they streaked barefoot through the woods for the lake, a dream that exploded when he tugged her with both hands in, in, in, past knee-high water, past waist-high water, in to over her head.

Life. God, what a burst of it! Her lazy lethargy totally disappeared. Her skin, suddenly cooled, turned vibrant and vital and tingly. She cleaved for the surface and clawed for air, exploding with energy, brimming with it, celebrating, high with it. Water trickled through her hair. Droplets shimmied down her forehead.

Jarl looked at her, threw back his head, and laughed.

And a woman not of this earth abruptly turned mortal. His sauna had been mystical magic; that was done. Reality was a crescent moon and a black, silent night, lake water like ice...and a man. A man with jet-black eyes and water streaming from his shoulders, a man breathing as hard as she was, a man who'd just taken her to another world and knew it. His laughter faded into a slow curve of a smile, an intimate smile, a sassy smile.

She reached for him. She didn't make a conscious decision, it was simply what happened. Her palms slid over his cool bare skin and felt his supple muscles contract. Abandoned, reckless, her mouth claimed his. Claim was the only emotion in her head. He was hers for this moment, because she desperately wanted and needed him. He'd given her so much and there was no way on earth she could believe this was wrong.

Water splashed up and displaced when she molded closer. Two heads showed in the moonlight. Shoulders and below were in another world, a liquid world where breasts, all slippery and tight, lay against his hard chest. Belly grazed belly, thighs courted thighs where no one could see. The slinky, icy water should have affected his ability to be aroused. It didn't. In some crazy corner in her mind, she told herself to remember that. Lord almighty, he turned on faster than the flip of a dime.

He also kissed with the delicious, wanton, forbidden temptation of sin. Her head reeled back under the pressure of his mouth. His lips rubbed against hers until she trembled. His tongue ravished and lavished attention on hers.

The erotic pull started in her toes and swept through her body, the night, the sky. A sensual awareness of her body had started in the sauna, but this was a sexual awareness that was huge, hot, raw and real. Jarl was so real: his skin and the taste of him, the feel of him against her abdomen. He kissed like he would set her lips on fire, then turned her upside down when he kissed with tenderness.

There was just Jarl. There had been no other men in her life. There had been no other life, until this instant, this man, this raw terrible softness and this yearning ache and this . . . power.

Jarl fought for control like a man drowning. She was so sweet! The sauna had never been about seduction, but about trust. He wanted her to know, from the soul, that her vulnerability was something he would protect, not hurt. The sauna was to relax her so she would talk to him.

But dammit she shouldn't have reached for him. He raised her waist-high out of the water so his lips could warmly nuzzle and tease her breasts. She tossed her head back, baring her throat, so white and vulnerable, in the moonlight. Her fingers curled and clutched when his tongue wooed the tips of her breasts. A sound whispered over the lake, coming from her throat, a helpless cry, a demand.

The sound shredded his sanity. He didn't care. He was coming apart at the seams. He didn't care. The rippling softness of her skin mattered, the wild silver glow of her eyes, the need he sensed in her to be loved. Now. Thoroughly. By him.

There was nothing he wanted to do more, but it couldn't be. She was trembling from passion, but also starting to shiver from cold. Serious cold.

He whispered murmurs in her ear, soft promises, earthy words in his native, rolled tongue. *Kissa*, she knew, but not *nainen*. He wanted her to do something. She didn't know what it was. Her whimpers told him that she felt disoriented when he started withdrawing kisses, afraid.

"Sssh, sssh." He scooped her up, still kissing her softly. He praised her for wanting him, for being wild and abandoned just for him, for not being able to walk, for being so loving. He praised her in Finnish because he knew he was praising her for irrational, silly things, and maybe, for things that mattered too much.

By the time they reached shore, she was shuddering with cold, blind with it. Her passion was gone but Sara was not quite Sara yet. He snatched the towel and rubbed it over her body, roughly, mercilessly. The shock from heat to cold directly from the sauna should be healthy and exhilarating, but too much heat, too much cold could make her ill. He was angry at himself that he'd risked her in any way.

"Jarl, slow down!"

"You *have* to get warm."

"But maybe you could leave me a layer of skin?"

Dark eyes met blue for a bare instant. Hers were calm, with a shy dance, a helplessness, an honesty. God, he loved her.

"You're not angry with me?" he said fiercely.

She shook her head.

"You don't regret this?"

She shook her head again.

He breathed in, out, with lungs starving for that relief. "I damn near took you standing up in the middle of the lake," he scolded her.

"Yes."

"That's not how I'm going to make love to you the first time."

He noticed the shadow that crossed her eyes.

Once he got her warm and dry and in the house, he intended to tackle that shadow. All her shadows.

Six

———

This will warm you up, Sara."

Sara glanced at the giant mug of Lakka he handed her. Warm her up? If she drank even half of it, she'd be comatose.

Being comatose had a certain appeal, and it would be far easier than trying to make sense of Jarl's behavior. Mutely she watched him crouch down and add sprigs of mint to the log fire. If Jarl hadn't been moving faster than a one-armed bandit the spit-crackling fire and wood scents and dark living room might have soothed her fractured nerves.

Less than an hour ago the two had shared a rage of emotions, come a hairsbreadth from making love, and experienced something so powerful and unexpected, special and terrifying that her pulse was still reeling from the impact.

Jarl was acting as if nothing had happened. Once he'd stashed her on the couch, swaddled fatter than a mummy in a bed blanket, he'd tugged on jeans, did whatever Finns do to saunas to shut them down, checked on Kip, poured her the liqueur and started the fire. Now he hung up the poker, adjusted the grate and smiled.

He'd smiled at her just that way when he'd walked up and stolen the shotgun out of her hands that first morning. His lips had an easy, innocuous curve. His dark eyes rested comfortably, naturally, on her face.

He'd fooled her then, but she tried hard not to make the same mistakes twice. Maybe she trusted him, but Jarl was sneaky. Just like a dangerous, unpredictable predator, he now loomed over her, pushed aside the blanket, and gently tugged her into the nook between his arm and body.

Damn the man.

She closed her eyes and rested her cheek on his bare shoulder. He smelled good, clean, woodsy and male. His lips nuzzled the crown of her head, which effectively mortgaged another few ounces of her common sense.

She knew she had to get up and do things, say things, that would defuse what had happened between them in the lake, but she felt so damn fragile. Fragile, shaky, and scared out of her mind.

She didn't know who had been making love to him in that cool, dark lake, but it couldn't have been her. Nightmares of police and custody hearings were her life. She never forgot that. Kip was her life. She never forgot her child. But now she was willing to concede that needs and passion and loneliness could be powerful stuff with the right man, a good man, a special lover. Her heart trumpeted that Jarl was all three. Her head knew darn well that no woman really climbed out of herself and shattered when a man kissed her, no matter who that man was.

She obviously needed a psychiatrist. Or a crowbar. Nothing less was going to pry her away from the warm curve of his body. What had he done to her?

"You're not drinking," he scolded.

Obediently she took a sip, hoping the drink would work as a bracer. It worked as an aphrodisiac, and all Jarl did was sift her drying hair between his fingers. "I need to bring up something awkward," he murmured.

"Awkward?" She set down the mug of Lakka, not looking at him. Like the superstition about not stepping on a crack, she hoped her brain would consider refunctioning if she was simply careful not to look at him.

He coiled a strand of her hair around a finger. "I was prepared, Sara. Not a very romantic subject, I know. But I can't have you thinking I'm the kind of man who would allow you to risk a pregnancy you weren't prepared for. When I met you, you were alone, obviously not anticipating involvement with anyone. I have, and have had, the means to protect you." Once that subject had been covered as casually as the weather, he shifted to another. "Why did you do it? Cut your hair?"

"My hair?" Like the chorus in a rock song, her pulse beat out he'd *known* they were going to be lovers. He'd known. He'd thought about birth control. She hadn't known or realized, and what happened to all the careful lectures she'd given him about being casual summer friends?

"Your hair," he repeated. "You used to wear it long— longer than your shoulders. And you wore it down, not twisted up or fancy. Whenever you're distracted, you raise your hand to push it back, the way a woman does when she's used to pushing back long hair from her face. The way you're doing now." He claimed the small hand en route to her shoulders, stroked the base of her palm with his thumb, and released it. "Why did you cut it?"

She was too rattled to produce more than a single word. "Because."

"Because why?"

"Jarl, we can't be lovers, and there'll be no more saunas."

He nodded, just like he'd nodded when he'd snatched the shotgun out of her hand that first morning.

"I know what nearly happened tonight. I know it must seem like I've led you on."

"You've never led me on, *kissa*."

Wrapping the blanket tighter around her, she groped for the right words. "I thought we'd talked. I thought you felt the same way I did. People meet on summer vacations. That's never the same as real life."

"No?"

"Of course not. Summers are lonely, the days are long, you're not around the normal people you know, doing the normal things you do. So it's easy to want someone to talk to, be with. But at the end of the summer, you go back to real life." For the first time she risked a glance at his face. His smile was mild and soothing, his eyes luminous. "Your hardware store is in Pontiac," she reminded him. "I don't live anywhere near there. I mean, it would be silly for us to get involved."

"Very silly," he agreed.

"Neither one of us wants to get serious."

"Of course we don't."

"A low-key friendship is a completely different thing."

"It certainly is."

"No questions, no complications."

"Ideal," Jarl murmured amiably. "No one risks getting hurt that way."

"Yes!" After the sauna, the lake, she never dreamed this would go so easily. Relief put a shine in her eyes; air rushed from her lungs in a long, low sigh. "Jarl, I wouldn't hurt you. Tell me if I've done anything to hurt you."

"Nothing, *nainen*."

She hesitated. "*Nainen?* You called me that before. What does it mean?"

He smiled. There were times Finnish didn't precisely translate into English. *Nainen* roughly translated into *my woman*, but there were implications of possessiveness and protectiveness that Sara, perhaps, was too American to appreciate. "You haven't finished your drink," he said, diverting her, "and you haven't told me why you cut your hair."

"I never cut my hair."

What a fibber she was. His smile broadened.

"And Jarl, about what happened at the lake...."

"I fell in love with you long before what happened to-night, *kissa*. What happened at the lake was as inevitable as sunshine and moonlight. It simply took you a little longer to see what we had."

With a flash of sparks a log fell into the bed of coals. Jarl eased to his feet and grabbed the poker. "I want your children, you know. Several of them. My lake cottage will still do for a summer home for years, but not my place in Pontiac, not once you and Kip move in and we start a family..."

"*Jarl.*"

Once the log was fixed, he replaced the grate, and dusted the soot from his hands. "We'll need a bigger place."

"You've got to stop this talk."

"I think I'll get a little drink. I wasn't thirsty before, but I'm getting there. We need to get just a few small things out of the way before the wedding, *nainen*. It would be nice if you'd get around to telling me your last name. And other little things. Whether you have relatives, how you happen to be on this island, why you're scared to leave it, what Kip's nightmares are about, and what on earth we're going to do about this very big trouble you're in." He paused in the kitchen doorway. "I'll be right back. You're not ready for a refill yet, are you?"

She was ready for a heart attack. The instant he was out of sight, she surged off the couch and nearly killed herself tripping over the blanket. Impatiently she gathered it up to fly after him. Her mug spilled. She left the mess. Frantic lies were trying to form on the tip of her tongue—some good, some bad, some wild, some she was still trying to invent faster than the speed of light.

She said nothing for a moment. A single oil lamp illuminated the shadowed kitchen. That yellow glow concentrated light on Jarl, where he was reaching for the second shelf cupboard where he kept his Lakka. He knew where his Lakka was; he knew where the glasses were. She had the sudden terrifying feeling that he knew where her heart was.

He loved her.

She'd never once considered that he'd fall in love with her.

Silly pictures flooded her head. Pictures of Kip on Jarl's lap in front of a Christmas tree. Pictures of his rumpled head on a pillow next to her in the morning. Pictures of the two of them arguing in a kitchen. Heavens, if she had Jarl full-time, they'd argue plenty. Some woman had to break him of this habit of ignoring what she said and listening only to his own drummer. Pictures of her pregnant. Pictures of her lying beneath him on rumpled sheets on hot summer nights, brazen bare, vulnerable, her skin slick, calling his name....

She loved him, too. But it just couldn't be.

Jarl poked the neck of the bottle into a small glass with Big Bird on it. He only poured a thumbfull, but the amber-red liquid still sloshed out of the bottle. His hands weren't steady. He reached for a kitchen cloth, trying to remember another time when his hands hadn't been steady. There wasn't another time. He'd never lived his life on that kind of edge.

He felt on edge now, when he turned, took three rapid gulps of his drink, and faced Sara. A look of rejection on her face would have been its own answer. He saw no rejection; he saw fear. She looked waif-like with the blanket draped over her shoulders. She leaned against the doorway as if gravity alone wouldn't hold her up. Her soft, spiked bangs were flying every which way and her tan battled with the pallor of stress. Pallor had won.

"In a normal courtship," he said quietly, "a man takes out a woman once a week. Twice? Usually for no more than a few hours at a time. So over a few months, that adds up to what? Thirty hours together, forty? So don't tell me we haven't known each other long enough, *kissa*. Tick off the hours and you'll know how much time we've spent together. I've seen you happy, sad, hungry, angry, exasperated, and so loving with your son. I've seen you beautiful. I've seen you when you were so tired you couldn't put one foot in front of another. You're strong and you're clever and you're a very passionate woman, *nainen*. And I'm going to know tonight, right now, exactly what you're afraid of."

"Sit."

Her short command raised a smile—his, not hers. And being Jarl, he didn't obey and sit but simply leaned back against the counter, ankles crossed, waiting. The floor was cold on her bare feet. She lifted up and perched on the table edge, not a chair.

Good sense came to her easily now, so did sharpened wits. Protecting people she loved was what Sara did best, and guilt tore at her, for a situation that was all of her making, all of her fault. She and Kip were locked in a no-win, no-answer life-style. Never mind what she wanted, what she needed, or what she felt for Jarl. Selfishness was unforgivable. She had no business drawing him into the dark web of her life.

She had to free him. Now. Jarl's dark eyes were waiting, fathomless, intense. Lying to him was suddenly as impossible as the truth, but a woman who cared enough, loved enough, could find a balance of both. "I need to tell you about Kip's father," she said quietly.

"Yes."

She turned away from his gravelly, seductive voice and focused on the pool of light next to him. "I didn't know when I married him that he had had an accident when he was very young. I had no reason to know it, no reason to think anything was wrong with him. In that accident, he suffered a head injury. Sometimes—not often at first and this was not something he could anticipate—he would suddenly change. Totally and completely change personality. He would get these dark moods, these rages..."

She lifted her head high. "We lived with his parents. Maybe that wasn't my choice when we were first married, but I didn't mind and it didn't seem so odd. I'd lost my parents, his cared tremendously for me and that went both ways. It was a huge house; there was lots of room for privacy. His parents should have told me about the accident. They didn't. And Kip was not planned, because by then I knew it wasn't the kind of marriage one should bring a child into. But Kip happened."

Ice shards lanced through his veins, maybe caused by her matter-of-fact voice. She was recounting facts. Too fast, too sharply, he was forming precise ugly images of exactly how Kip had been conceived, exactly what kind of marriage Sara had survived.

"When Kip's father was...himself...he was a good man in all kinds of ways, and I thought—I made the mistake of believing—that between my husband's parents and myself, I could protect my son. When I discovered that wasn't possible, I divorced him."

She had to stop for an instant. It had always been hard to lie to Jarl; now she found it was even harder to tell him the truth.

Everything she'd told him so far had been dead true, but the last time she'd told the truth it had been turned against her. She'd had no proof. People like their truth coated with proof. In the courtroom, it had almost seemed funny to hear herself called unreliable and unbalanced and burdened with mood swings, when it was Derek with the real problem and every Chapman witness knew it.

Why should Jarl believe her now? The judge hadn't, and she was tired of "truth." Her tone lowered, as soft as despair. "Jarl, my whole priority in life is my son right now. This whole summer is to give him time. Time to be just a little boy, with no worries and no pressures, time to erase bad memories for him and build a family of two that he knows he can count on."

When Jarl took a step toward her, she raised her hand. "No! You've got to listen, honestly listen this time." Her fingers fretfully tugged at the blanket. "I could tell you I loved you. It wouldn't make any difference. I will not be involved right now, not with you, not with anyone."

"Kissa—"

She shook her head, fiercely, angrily, the words coming fast now. "I owe my son. I owe him stability. I owe him my undivided time and commitment. It's not a joke, what he's been through." Before it was too hard she added, "I want you—*need* you—to walk out of my life. I want you to find someone else. Everything I have to give as a human being, a woman, goes to my son right now. That's the way it has to be. That's the way I want it. I have absolutely nothing to offer you."

"Sssh. So upset. How could you believe I wouldn't respect how you feel for your son?" This time when he surged forward, he ignored her outstretched hand. His palms cupped her face, raised it. She was white like paper, fragile like crystal, shaky like starbeams. A man didn't wage war with a woman that vulnerable.

Soft as a buttercup, his lips brushed hers. Her whole body froze in stillness, but her soft red lips parted willingly under his. "You want me to go?"

"Yes."

When she opened her eyes, he was gone.

Two days later the heat wave broke with a noisy, crashing thunderstorm. The morning was dark as dusk. A blustery wind hurled spears of gray rain at the windows. The small fire in the hearth took the dampness from the living room, but the flames spit and hissed every time a drop of water made it down the chimney. Kip's nose was flattened to a window. "It's almost stopped. We can swim."

"It's thunder and lightning, and no, we can't swim."

"I could put a raincoat over my swimsuit."

"That just won't help, punkin. How about a game of old maid or fish?"

"I don't want to play cards. I want to swim, Mom."

"Believe me, you've made that very clear." How many times had she prayed Kip would withdraw from his shell and become fractious and ornery and normal four-year-old-tempered if she loved him enough? Lord knew she loved him, but this morning her son was proving as impossible to entertain as a cooped-up bear. "Come on, let's set up our easels and have a finger-painting contest."

When she peeled him away from the window, he shot her a glare as ferocious as the thunderclouds. "Where's Jarl? Jarl would let me swim. He hasn't been here in two whole days."

"Jarl would not let you swim in a lightning storm."

"He would, too!"

"Honey, I told you from the first, Jarl is just a friend, not someone we can see every day. He doesn't live on the lake all the time; he has another place. He also has a store in another city."

"I don't care about his old store."

"I know you don't." He cared about seeing Jarl, and she didn't know how to tell him that possibly Jarl wasn't coming back. Ever, ever, ever. Her heart pounded that litany.

"And I hate rain!"

She was beginning to hate it, too. Absently she leaned down and pushed at the hem of her jeans. All morning the fabric had been scraping an odd sore spot on her ankle. She saw an inch-long cut, all red and puffy. She must have nicked her leg shaving on the dock the day before.

What did it matter? She straightened again, staring at the wild wind and broody sky, the silver slashes of rain drumming rhythms on the window panes. She kept telling herself that she was glad she'd finally chased Jarl out of their lives. She had been irresponsible and selfish and reckless to let him come as close as he had.

She knew everything she'd risked, everything she'd done wrong, but it didn't seem to help. She missed him. Her heart felt mournful and achy.

"Mom, I am bored."

Her son deserved better than a sad-sack mom. "I know you are, love." She threw cheer and enthusiasm in her voice. "And we're going to take care of that right now." Efficient and quick, she set up the easels, clipped on shiny paper, and searched for the fingerpaint.

She was coaxing Kip to find his paint shirt when she heard a knock on the door. Before surprise could even register, Max strode in, his head as wet as his cigar, water slushing off his yellow rainslicker. "Day ain't even fit for ducks," he barked.

"Max! You didn't bring out supplies in this weather? And you weren't even due until tomorrow!"

"Yeah, yeah. Well, what else was I going to do on a morning like this but drink too much coffee and wait for customers who aren't coming? And I brought something for the boy." Max's eyes drilled into Sara's, both aware that although Kip had instantly bolted for his mom's side, he hadn't disappeared from sight. "Well, now." Max looked at him again. "Well, now. The earth ain't caved in and here we are in the same room. Imagine that."

His lips curved in a giant smile as he dragged off his slicker, then he started patting pockets, first his shirt pockets, then his pants. Nothing. He bent over, huffing a little, and miraculously produced a giant sucker from the cuff of his serge overalls.

He held it out. When Kip didn't budge, Max sighed, but as soon as he laid the sucker on the table, Kip sprang for it.

"Thanks!"

With one guilty look at Sara, the urchin was gone, taking the stairs to his room two at a time with his booty.

"Sugar," Sara scowled at his benefactor.

"Did you hear him? The kid just said thanks."

"We have discussed sugar before."

"Yeah, yeah. You gotta quit reading those books. The kid doesn't even know what a sugar high is. What kind of upbringing is that? Besides, he talked to me. To hell with the coloring books. Next time I'm bringing him fifty pounds of chocolate."

"You do and your life won't be worth a Las Vegas dollar."

"So you say. You gonna make me a cup of coffee or do I have to beg for it?"

"I'll make you some herbal tea with milk."

He made a face. Kip made the same face when Sara fed him cough medicine. Chuckling, needing Max's company more than he knew, Sara padded in stockinged feet toward the kitchen to set a pot on the stove. By the time she brought him a steaming mug, he'd hunched over a chair by the fire. The tip of a white envelope peeked out from under a driftwood centerpiece on the mantel."

"What's that?"

"Nothin'. Something you can open when I'm gone."

She opened it now because she knew him. Once she read the words of ownership on the deed, she handed it back to him with a firm frown. "No, Max. We've discussed this before."

"Yeah, and you don't listen. I'm sixty-seven years old. I got my bait shop, I got my house. I got nothing to do with my money and if I want to give you the island, I'll give you the island. What am I supposed to do with the damn thing at my age?"

"I'm not broke. I've told you before what I got as a lump sum from the divorce—"

"Enough to fill a baby's piggy bank."

"I had jewelry to sell. And I'm being paid for these illustrations."

"Okay, okay, you got a fat fortune in sold baubles. Now you got an island to add to it. Cripes, I'm drinking your tea, aren't I? Don't give me a hard time." He added gruffly, "Taxes paid three years up. Course the government'll up the tax rate and then you'll be stuck with the difference."

She seemed doomed to love men who failed to listen to her. "Max, I will not let you do this."

"You win." He changed directions with shrewd speed. "Rain or no rain, I got eyes. Thought I'd wandered onto a completely different island this morning. Repaired roof, repaired dock. The backyard's beginning to look golf-course fancy. Somebody trimmed the dead wood out of the peaches, and there's this strange-looking structure outside."

"A sauna," Sara answered, quickly becoming aware that her caretaker had come to pry. Truthfully, she'd expected it before this.

"Imagine that. A sauna," Max repeated in his best amazed voice. He lifted his cigar, reached for a lighter, then waited patiently for Sara to reach over and pluck it out of his hand. Her back was turned for bare seconds when she plopped the lighter on the mantel. Long enough for him to slide the white envelope under the chair cushion. "Wouldn't be a Finnish sauna, would it?"

"Unless someone recently constructed a high rise in front of your bait shop window, my best guess is that you already know how often Jarl's been here." Sara's tone was wry.

"Yup. Same as set up housekeeping, far as I could tell," Max said amiably. "On the other hand, you didn't send off the pigeons. Anything really wrong, I figured you'd send off an SOS."

Max had supported her and encouraged her and loved her, and she wished she could smile for him. Max deserved smiles but she simply couldn't pretend she could handle this subject lightly. "There was no need for an SOS," she said quietly. "That first morning, he shook me, I admit it. Maybe I didn't handle that so well, but in the long run, well, you know me, Max. I can do whatever I have to do."

"Managed to finally discourage him, did you?"

"Of course. Not fast enough, but I couldn't help that. In the beginning, I was afraid to be too unfriendly, too different, for fear he'd be curious about us. And then... But it doesn't matter. He's gone now. There was never any other choice."

Max viewed her fragile profile when she knelt at the hearth to fuss with the fire that was doing just fine without help. While she fooled with the poker, he silently filched a box of matches from his pocket and lit his cigar. "Since I saw he was over so much, I happened to do some extra checking on him."

"It doesn't matter now."

He nodded, his teeth clamping down on the cigar. It was pretty damn obvious that nothing in hell mattered now. "The boy's done some big changing since I saw him last."

She poked a log, staring at the flying sparks. "He was good with Kip," she admitted softly.

"Kind of had to be a special man, if he won over the tyke."

"He is."

"Ain't everybody you'd let close to your son. Musta done something to earn your trust."

Regrettably, Sara chose that moment to glance up. Max got in two fast puffs before she shot to her feet, stole the cigar and tossed it in the flames. He shot her a baleful glance that should have raised a fast, sassy line out of her. He got nothing.

"Well, now..." Max pleated his fingers over his stomach and stretched out his legs. "I guess it's a real good thing you rousted him before he settled in too close. Especially if you didn't trust him."

"I never said I didn't trust him!" She threw herself in the chair, restless, weary. The sore on her leg bothered her. A chipped nail bothered her. Everything was bothering her that normally didn't, and for what? For nothing. She just felt like baying at the moon like a hound. "Trust has nothing to do with anything, Max. For heaven's sake! I'm wanted by the police. There's a judge in Detroit who claims I'm an unfit, abusive mother. I could trust Jarl from here to Poughkeepsie, but I'm certainly not going to let him tie up with two people in as big a mess as we're in!"

"You didn't tell him anything, then?"

"Of course not!"

"Maybe you should."

She shook her head swiftly. "Never."

"Never's the longest word I know. The island won't work forever, Sara. We always talk like it will. We both know it won't. You got me as long as I'm able, but I got a flipper for a ticker and I'm gettin' older by the day. You need another answer besides me."

"Nothing's going to happen to you," Sara said fiercely. "I won't let anything happen to you."

"And Kip? What happens the first time the tyke gets a toothache, or sprains his little finger, or—"

"Nothing's going to happen to Kip either. I won't let anything happen to Kip!" Sara heard the blind desperation in her voice and fell silent. Jerking out of the chair, she pushed at her hair. She glanced at the stairs and then she glared back at Max. "What's gotten into you? You know I can't tell Jarl. You know I can't tell anyone. You've always been the first to agree with me."

"I know, short stuff." Max couldn't keep his eyes off her face. "But maybe I was wrong. Maybe I never thought out how the whole thing might change if you found a man who'd love you, someone you trusted, someone who'd help."

"Max." Her tone had a hopeless burr, defeated, lost. "Jarl can't help me. No one can. I can't ask someone to share my life as long as we're living this way, and we're always going to live this way because I'm never going back. Have you forgotten? The legal system locked up my son for seven months with a madman. I had attorneys. I worked with Friend of the Court. I had the testimony of two doctors and a psychiatrist. None of it made any difference."

He hated the haunted look in her eyes. "Honey, I know that," he said placatingly. "The Chapmans have got money and they've got power and they want their grandson. But they can't buy every judge. If you get someone else on your side, someone who knows you—"

She shook her head. To involve Jarl was to hurt him. The Chapmans would just take him down, too. He had a store, security, a life. They could threaten all of that—and would.

Derek's parents could do anything they pleased except, she remembered bitterly, protect one small boy from their troubled son.

She rarely thought of the night she'd stolen Kip from the Chapman house. Now memories clutched at her like a nightmare. She'd waited one night too many. She'd wanted an evening when her ex-in-laws were out. They'd finally been out. The only one in the house was Derek, sleeping like the dead the way he always slept after one of his "problem moods."

Even knowing the Chapmans' security system, breaking into the house had been its own bad dream, but the worst had been initially failing to find her son. He hadn't been in his bed, but in a closet, curled up like a fetus in a womb. He hadn't said a word when she found him, just clawed his arms around her neck, mute, tearless, blind with terror.

She pushed aside the memory, knowing it would make her physically ill if she didn't. Her gaze pinned Max. He'd always supported her, not because he thought she was right but because he loved her. Once, he'd teased her about being as blind and stubborn as a brick wall.

He was right where her son was concerned—where anyone she loved was concerned.

She leaned over to kiss the grooves on his forehead. "You can just quit worrying," she scolded him. "I don't need Jarl, Max. I don't need anyone. I'll take care of my own."

Seven

Two days later, midafternoon, Jarl threw a line at her dock, wrapped it, and beelined for her house.

She wasn't there, but she had been. A woman's tennies had been deserted on the veranda by Kip's, and from there it was simply a matter of following a Hansel-and-Gretel trail. They'd lunched in the yard and left crusts for the birds. Twenty feet toward the peach orchard, a toy crane had momentarily abandoned a stone-hauling project.

He found a half-filled bushel, also abandoned, which made sense when he scooped up a peach and tasted it. Rock-hard and bitter. Her orchard was weighed down with the nectar-sweet scent of ripening peaches. The fruit was fuzz-soft and big and pretty, just a week from being edible . . . and his two were nowhere in sight or sound.

He tossed away the peach and ducked under the low-hanging branches, heading for the knoll at the far side of the island. Overhead, clouds bunched, then dispersed, bunched, then dispersed. When the sun poured down, it was fiercely hot. When it disappeared, it was shade cool.

Halfway to the crest of the mini-dune, he saw two small legs chugging toward him with the speed of a locomotive.

"Jarl! Where have you been?"

"Hi, sport." Kip was all sand, all jellied cheeks, all sunburned grin. Without thinking or needing to think, Jarl swooped him up on an arm. "Where's your mom?"

Kip motioned vaguely behind him toward the beach. "I had a million things to ask you and you weren't here," he said reproachfully.

"I am now. What's to ask?" The weight of the little one didn't begin to slow him down.

"Can squirrels swim?"

"Nope."

"Then how come we have squirrels on the island? How could squirrels be on an island if they can't swim?"

"There's a sandbar in the lake, Kip. And in the winter the water's so shallow there that it freezes over. A squirrel or a rabbit could walk across if they wanted to. And I guess they must have wanted to, because you have squirrels and rabbits on the island."

"Okay. I have another question," Kip announced.

Actually, he had another half dozen. Jarl answered, but every muscle strained and puckered when he glimpsed the caramel-tossed head down the beach. "How's our turtle, half-pint?"

"Wonderful. Want me to go get him?"

"I sure do."

The little one wriggled out of his arms and flew. So did Jarl, but not in the same direction.

His lady was lying on the sand in cotton jeans and a red shirt. The closer he came, the more blood pumped to his heart. He knew why he'd stayed away for four days. He also knew why he'd come back.

His boots made distinct, heavy prints in the sand, but no sound. He didn't want her to hear him. His senses were privately greedy for the look of her. His gaze lapped up the sight of her sandy toes, the curve and length of cotton-clad thighs, the way her breasts flattened into two small mounds under the gathered top. Her throat was bare, vulnerable. A drop of moisture had collected in the hollow of her throat like a crystal. Another row of crystals made a necklace on her temples.

He was nearly on top of her before she stirred. Her eyes popped open, smudge-blue and disoriented. Again tension tightened the corded muscles down his spine, but not in wariness at her discovering him. With her eyes open, he saw the shadows of exhaustion and a pallor beneath her sun-gold skin. She wasn't waking from a sun-bathing doze, but from a drugging nap.

His eyes sharpened on her face. Sara didn't nap. She also didn't sunbathe. And though her son swam like a fish, she never allowed Kip near the water unless she was there to watchdog everything he did. For her to have fallen asleep... but his concern never had a chance to secure a foothold.

The moment she was aware of him, she jerked up to a sitting position. He was braced for rejection, anger, hurt. Instead, he felt the burn of her eyes on his face. Moisture spiked the bangs on her brow. He saw love that sucked him in like champagne through a straw, and for the first time in ninety-six hours, he breathed.

Sara watched him drop down beside her. He lazily leaned back, using his arm for a pillow, and closed his eyes against the sudden wicked glare of sun. Dizziness swept through her. She pushed absently at her leg, aware of an annoying, hot pain near her ankle. He was here. He couldn't be. She didn't want him here. She did. She wanted everything she felt around Jarl—the stress and exhilaration, the anxiety and simmering softness, the hopelessness, the sweet helpless need—over with. She'd thought it was over with. If he just hadn't come back... but he had.

The heat had her pulse beating exulting rhythms. All day the heat had been doing crazy things to her. She felt muzzy and limp and strange. Nothing was normal, nothing was right, yet now she felt miraculously better. The sensations of weakness and warmth were welcomed. So was her silly giddiness. The weight of the Egyptian pyramids had just been lifted off her heart.

"I was pretty sure..." Her tongue felt freshly coated with dryness. She stopped pushing at her leg and focused blindly on the painfully bright dance of sun on water. "I was pretty sure you weren't coming back."

"I was always coming back. It just took me a little time to stop being furious with you."

"Furious?" His voice was a melting baritone; she didn't hear any anger.

He had in mind a slow buildup to a serious talk, but Kip wasn't going to take forever to find a box turtle. Sand scratched his spine where he burrowed in. "I wasn't sure what to do about you, *nainen*. I haven't been sure what to do about you from the day I met you. My life is ten-penny nails and T pipes. Everything is logical, everything is in its place. Then I meet a woman who turns me on like I'm a teenage boy again. A woman who is stubborn like a mule, a woman who can't cook fish. I could build a barn faster than I can coax smiles out of this woman, and she has worked desperately hard to throw me out of her life from the first day I met her. I'm still damn mad," he told her.

"You don't sound mad."

"Of course I don't sound mad. Do you think I would get mad at a woman?" He opened his eyes to glare at her, but the sun dazzled his expression into his squint.

So far, he hadn't said much that was reasonable. That was all right. She didn't feel so reasonable either. She saw the drape of sun and shadow on his bare shoulders, the length of strong muscles covered in dark jeans. She saw his eyes. She was hot and dizzy and strangely shaky. His lying next to her was right. Lord, she missed him.

His voice turned low, quiet, serious. "I was angry with you because I wanted you to tell me the truth and you lied." When she immediately started to protest, he raised his hand to her lips.

"I know, *nainen*—you told me the truth about your ex-husband, about your feelings for your son. That came through in your eyes, your face, everything about you. But you know how I feel about your son. You must know know I'd harm myself before I'd harm Kip, so to use him to avoid a relationship between us is a lie. A natural lie, I told myself, if the lady is that damn sure she wants me out of her life. So I spent four days asking myself whether I needed to get kicked in the teeth. Why don't I simply respect the lady's choices and let the whole thing go?''

The sun was still blinding him when he leaned forward and brushed a strand of hair from her cheek. Her skin felt burning hot. She carried the scent of peaches. He could taste her fragility. She looked too damn small and too damn troubled. ''There's a reason why I came back. I can handle the words in Finnish, but those you wouldn't understand. You have an American song—there's a phrase—you are the wind beneath my wings. That's why I came back, *kissa*. And don't try arguing with me. I'm not leaving you again.''

She stared at him, mesmerized, aching, silky warm from the inside out. She knew the emotion he was talking about. It was exactly what she felt when she was with him. Still she managed a whispered, ''No.''

''Yes.''

''No.''

''Against all my better judgment, we will do it your way,'' he consoled her. ''I won't ask you why you won't leave the island, what you're afraid of, why you won't do anything so simple as row across the lake and see my house and have dinner with me. I have, as of now, not noticed any of those things.''

He wanted to say more. He wanted to honestly admit he refused to play that insane game for an infinite period of time, but he spotted Kip scuttling down the sandy knoll in the distance. The sun ducked behind a cloud as he immediately lurched to a sitting position. Solar glare no longer blinding him, he had a fresh look at her face. Emotions were tabled promptly. ''Hey. What is all this?''

Softer than a wisp of cotton, his thumbs brushed the dark shadows under her eyes. ''Nothing.''

"You haven't been sleeping?"

"I'm fine, Jarl." Her state of health was the last thing on her mind. She, too, saw Kip. She had told Max that she could take care of her own, and meant it. She could take care of her son, and any minute now she was going to find the strength and energy to find some way to take care of this man who was so dear to her. Everything he'd said had made her love him. Everything he'd said had frightened her.

Strength—mental, emotional and physical—had never been so important. Yet for that precise instant, it took every ounce of energy she possessed to simply get to her feet.

"What is wrong?" Jarl said harshly.

"Nothing. Honest. Nothing." She threw him a reassuring smile, all she could do, and then Kip descended on them with a mournful tale about an escaped turtle.

Jarl pushed himself to a standing position, opened his mouth and abruptly closed it. She had smiles and animated conversation for her son. Perhaps he'd imagined her stark white color when she stood up. Possibly she was simply tired. Lord knew, he was. Possibly she was pale and slightly physically out of sorts because it was a delicate time of the month for her. Questions that were natural between a man and a woman were set aside because of a three-foot-two-inch listener with big ears. And neither exhaustion nor feminine complaints meant that she was ill.

"Jarl?" A small hand tugged at his jeans pocket. "You too old to play hide-and-seek?"

Hide-and-seek? He pushed his fingers through the little one's mop of hair. He loved Kip more than anything, but at the moment he really wanted to be alone with Kip's mother.

"Please? Please, Jarl? You're not too old, are you?"

"No one's too old for hide-and-seek."

"So let's go! Didn't you hear? Mom said she'd be it—we gotta get to the peach orchard. She'll never find us there!"

He shot a lingering look at Sara. Half amused, half exasperated, he said, "I'm not done with you, *nainen*."

"Count, Mom!"

"One. Two. Three...." There was a brief hesitation, but then he took her son, and she heard them racing and laughing through the brush toward the orchard. For one sparse second she wanted nothing more than to curl herself into a small ball.

"Four. Five. Six..." The sun was too bright. Pain sneaked in front of her eyes everywhere she turned. Something seemed wrong with her, terribly wrong. It was far more than Jarl coming back, more than Jarl not coming back, more than her insurmountable problems. "Nine. Ten!"

She wanted to sleep, not play, yet an emotional momentum gave her the physical strength to climb after them. The peel of Kip's laughter was a powerful stimulus. He was laughing... because Jarl was there.

Every muscle and nerve fought her at first. She coaxed them into cooperating. She found herself picking up speed, ducking and dodging between trees, calling out threats to the first body she found and, yes, laughing. Was it because Jarl was there? She needed strength and answers to do the right thing for Jarl, but the game was so silly, so harmless. How could she think a simple game of hide-and-seek could pose danger to any of them? And it was easy to find them. Kip considered himself hidden if his head was out of sight. Jarl's dark jeans were a beacon in the orchard.

Finding them was easy, but catching them something else. The ripening peaches smelled overpoweringly, dazzlingly sweet. The old trees were built funny, each with a tiny, squatty trunk and then millions of knife-shaped leaves forming umbrellas at eye level. Branches bit and scraped her bare shoulders. She didn't care. Sun blazed in her eyes, then shadows, sun, then shadows, like a kaleidoscope turning at dizzying speeds.

She tripped once, and felt a spear of white-hot pain shoot directly into her skull, shocking her, disorienting her. She couldn't let it take control. After this there could be no more play. After this she had to get rid of that man if she did it with a shotgun. After this there could be no more lazy, shimmering afternoons, no more playing, no more feeling the sizzle and rush and crazy high of being near him.

She wanted to run. She wanted to run forever. If she could just keep on running, didn't breathe, didn't stop, didn't think, didn't feel . . . if she just kept on running, she could love him.

It didn't seem logical at all to have a wave of hot blackness clamp down on her head, to feel suddenly wet all over. The trees were tipping. Silly, silly trees.

"Sara!"

Foolish man. Didn't he know the rules? He wasn't supposed to be running toward her. He was supposed to be hiding. She tried to tell him. He wasn't being very nice. His hands clutched painfully on her shoulders just as she felt herself sinking.

That wasn't how you played the game, and she suddenly wasn't running at all but staring up at a million peaches and thinking, the foolish trees. They hid all the peaches under the leaves where you couldn't see them from the outside. Even the peaches were playing hide-and-seek.

"Honey, where are you hurting?" He bent over her, sweeping his hands over her forehead, throat, wrists. Her pulse was as fast as a freight train. The heat he'd mistaken for sun was fever. Her eyes were a glaze of hectic sapphire fire.

He'd felt panic when he saw her falling. The panic was done, as inappropriate as guilt for not guessing earlier how ill she was. Panic and guilt were put on hold. What mattered was action, but moving her could be dangerous if he didn't have some idea what was wrong.

"Jarl, she's okay. She's just falling asleep again."

Jarl jerked his head to Kip, forced himself to swallow the grit in his throat and speak gently. "Your mom fell asleep before like this?"

"Two times this morning. She's just tired, Jarl. She told me."

"We'll take care of her," Jarl said soothingly, but loud, abrasive alarm bells jangled in his head.

"I already fixed her this morning. There's nothing to take care of, I told you. She's okay."

"Fixed what?"

"Her leg. I put the Band-Aid on."

Faster than lightning, he peeled up the cotton hem of her jeans. The material fit too closely to her calves to peel far, but he could raise it far enough to see the small, clean bandage, and when he ripped it off, the thick smudge of white first-aid cream. The cream didn't begin to disguise the huge, swollen, angry sore. He didn't need a doctor to recognize a serious infection, or to realize that the streaked red line climbing toward her knee meant blood poisoning.

Kip took one look at Jarl's face. His blithe confidence faltered, and then he zoomed to his feet. "I know what to do, Jarl. I know what to do. I'll take care of everything!"

Faster than wind he raced through the trees, through the yard, around the side of the house. He dragged over a pail to stand on, flipped open one cage. He dragged the pail to the next cage, and flipped it open. One, two, three, then all of them. In seconds all of the homers were free.

Jarl, he figured, was going to be unbeatably proud of him.

Sara didn't wake up for quite a while. One moment her eyes were closed, the next open, but the dream of vibration and fire kept going. Pain. Everyone knew pain. There was the pain of a cut and the pain of a toothache and stretched-muscle pain. This was the choking kind, like someone was twisting a red-hot knife in her ankle.

The motion and vibration made her think of riding in a car, which was obviously ridiculous. She couldn't be in a car, and where was Kip? She tried to move but couldn't. The blanket was too hot, but she seemed to be strapped into it.

All she could think of was that they'd found her. They were going to take Kip away from her again. Faces swirled in front of her eyes: the judge and the Chapmans and their attorneys. *Subject to unstable moods and fits of depression. We recommend no visitation rights, your honor. No visitation rights.* "It's them. Can't you see how clever they are? They twisted it all up; it was never me. You can't believe them, you can't; I'm telling you the truth." She never realized she was crying out.

"Sara."

Jarl's low baritone sliced through the fire, but God, she couldn't breathe. "I want my son!"

"Kip is fine and with Max—"

"He can't be with Max; he's afraid of Max. I want my—"

"Sssh. Sssh." With his foot jammed on the accelerator, he could only risk a quick glance over his shoulder. She was still securely tied. An ambulance would have been the better choice if there had been any time, but too much time had already been wasted getting her off the island. "Stay still, Sara. Absolutely still. Kip is fine. Max is fine. And you're going to be fine very soon, but you have to stay still. Sleep, *kissa.*"

"You can't let them have him!"

"No one is going to get your son."

"Promise me. Promise me."

"I promise you."

The next thing she was aware of was Jarl's long, strong arms lifting her from the back seat. White lights flashed. She heard the skid of wheels, the snatch of voices, the whir of an electric door opening. Someone foolishly tried to take Jarl away from her.

Alcohol smells bombarded her nose. She was raised onto something cold, white and hard. The sound of wheels in motion made her nauseous, harsh lights kept blinking above her, a needle was jabbed into her arm. Someone, again, tried to take Jarl away from her.

Snip, snip, snip. The blade of a cold scissor skimmed up her leg. Someone drew a curtain. Someone with soft brown eyes bent over her, disappeared.

"Do you happen to know if she's allergic to any medications, Mr. Hendriks?"

"I have no idea."

"Do you have any knowledge whether she had a recent tetanus vaccination?"

"I don't know."

"All right. There's a waiting room just down the corridor. You'll have to leave now. Before you go to the waiting room, stop at the desk for the admitting forms."

They were trying to do it again. Her fingers clutched his wrist with blind, violent strength. She tried to say his name once, but her vocal chords failed to function. She wasn't letting him go. She was getting used to the nightmare. Used to the pain, used to the black, to the fire, to the fear, to hallucinations and helplessness. Hell was knowing there was absolutely nothing that she was capable of doing, physically, emotionally, mentally. But she was not letting him go.

"You have to leave now, Mr. Hendriks."

The nurse's voice was growing strident. Jarl's fierce dark eyes bent over her, for the moment all she saw and all she knew. She had a thousand things to tell him, all desperately important, none that would wait, but it was so hard to push words past her throat. She whispered, "I love you."

His cool palm swept her forehead. "I love you, too. You're going to be fine, Sara. You think I'd let anything happen to you?"

"Mr. Hendriks, we can't begin surgery until someone has filled out the permission and admitting forms—"

Immediately he loosened her hold on his wrist, though she clutched at him. "Don't, Jarl. Don't fill out any forms. Don't tell them my name. And Kip. Get Kip. Not . . . with Max. Only with you. And I can't be here. I can't be here. I have to get out of here. I have to . . ."

She woke up saying the same thing. "I have to get out of here. Get Kip. For God's sake, get Kip."

"I have him, *nainen*. And I have you. Everything's fine." Jarl lurched up from the chair to push the nurse's button above her bed.

One square window decorated the recovery room, offering a view of a black, still night. Inside, there was too much white: the sheets, the walls, the thin cotton blanket covering her. Everything was white except for her two burning blue eyes.

The nurse stepped into the room, threw Jarl a wary glance, and reached for Sara's pulse. He'd torn the first strip off her when he'd walked into the room and found Sara alone. Four hours later, and there had been several rounds about rules. She was in no hurry to breathe too hard. A dropped pin was enough to set him off again. "I see she's awake," the nurse said, in the careful tone one would use in the same cage with a sleeping tiger.

"She's in pain. Do something. Now."

"I told you, Mr. Hendriks. We can't give her pain medication until her blood pressure stabilizes."

"Is it?"

"Yes, she's doing just fine now—"

"So move. Either give her something for the pain or I'll find a doctor who will. And I don't mean five minutes from now."

The nurse started to say something, then checked herself. She left and then there was just Sara's eyes staring at him, mute with betrayal, glazed, hurting. His own softened. "Don't try to talk again, *kissa*." He fussed with her sheet and pillow, clumsy as a bear in a dollhouse. His hands were too big, too rough, next to her porcelain fragility. Still, he needed to touch her.

"I have to talk." Her tongue felt wrapped in cotton. "Jarl, you have to get me out of here. Now. I have to get my son. I can't stay here."

"Sweetheart, there is no chance in hell you belong anywhere else. You can run the four-minute mile tomorrow, but today is definitely not your day. I'll have you home very soon, and you are never shaving your legs again as long as you live, did I tell you that?"

"Did you tell them my name?"

"Of course I did, Jane Smith." A flash of exasperation flared in his eyes. For Sara, he banked the anger. He wasn't angry with her anyway. He wasn't sure who he was mad at, only that the rage had started building the moment a woman in a white uniform had handed him a form and a pen.

Insurance numbers he left blank. He had no idea what coverage she had or didn't have, and it hardly mattered since he intended to write a check for the medical service. It was the other empty lines that caused the problem.

For no rational reason on earth, he'd found himself blithely and automatically scribbling in a Jane Smith at an invented address with an imaginary driver's license number. He'd sat there, a man who never lied, a man who never budged from the cliff of honesty, and watched himself fib with the skill of a poker player. Only he never played poker. And he never sold out on a principle. Men who liked to live with themselves were smarter than that.

He'd lied, knowing Sara's hysterical plea had come from the hallucination of fever. Hysteria and hallucinations weren't his problem. The gut instinct that she was not out of her mind had torn at him.

It still did. He could see what shape she was in. Pain leached the color from her lips, her eyes were on fire with it. She had no more stamina than a candle in the wind. Still, she tried to push up with a strength that had to come from her soul. God knows, her body had none. "We have to get to Kip."

Again, he tried the soothing, the rational. "Kip is fine and so are you. You'll be out of here in twenty-four hours if you rest."

"Twenty-four hours. No!" She caught his wrist with her fingers. She caught his heart with her eyes. "Help me."

"Sweetheart—"

"I have to get out of here. I have to get my son. It won't wait, and I can't do it without you. Jarl, please. Help me."

"*Nainen*, you are just out of surgery."

"Please."

"There is no way I am taking you outside at three o'clock in the morning in the shape you're in."

"Please."

He dragged a hand through his hair, glaring down at her, aware of the waves of exhaustion assaulting his tight muscles, a headache, a gnawing, churning stomach and eyes red from lack of sleep. He felt as if he was dealing with her four-year-old son, who could be stubborn, bullheaded and single-minded. He couldn't remember when she'd ever said "please." He couldn't stand the way she was looking at him.

He started moving toward the metal closet that held her clothes. "I'll get you out of here."

"Now."

"I'll get you out now. I'll get you out, I'll get your son, I'll get your Max. I'll take care of your damn island, and when this is all over, I may just shake you until your teeth rattle, *nainen*."

She saw his fiercely angry face looming over her. She'd never seen or imagined Jarl so angry, yet the kiss he brushed on her brow was as soft as spring.

She needed no other reassurance. She closed her eyes.

Eight

———

Whoa." Jarl stopped the speeding bullet with his bare hand.

"I want my mom, Jarl."

"I know you do, sport, and she's just as frantic to see you. But she has a real bad hurt on her leg, so we're not going to bounce on her. Anybody going in there who isn't real quiet and real gentle has to eat broccoli for the rest of their lives. Are we clear?"

They were clear. Jarl released the squirming boy, and pointed in the direction of the back bedroom. Kip flew past, and Jarl's eyes raised abruptly to the whiskered old man still standing in the doorway. "Come in."

"The tyke was kinda anxious to see her."

"I could see that."

Max wasn't half as anxious to cross Jarl's threshold. He was pleating his cap between his fingers as he stepped in. A cigar was clamped between his teeth like he wanted to bite it off.

The old man had reason to be nervous. Until two days ago Jarl had only known Max as the tattooed, shady-eyed codger who owned the bait shop. The afternoon Sara had been hurt, Max had arrived by boat at the same time Jarl had been carrying Sara to his. For the second time in a month Jarl had had a shotgun aimed at his nose, this time by a man who knew how to use the weapon, and intended to.

If Jarl had had time for patience, he might have tried arguing. He didn't have time. He was taking Sara, via his boat and then via his car, to a hospital. Nothing and no one was going to stop him.

They'd come to terms, after a brief battle over Kip. Jarl had wanted him, and the boy was clearly anxious around Max. But the old man showed sense there. Kip belonged with him. There was no way Jarl could logically handle both Kip and Sara in a hospital setting.

Much later, the obvious occurred to Jarl. Max had to be the man with the homers, the man who was the key to their supplies on the island, the man who knew the whole nature of the trouble Sara and Kip were in. Max had answers. Then, though, there had been no time to wring them out of him.

Now there was time and the old coot knew it, because he was looking everywhere but Jarl's face. "How is she?"

"Now that her son's here, hopefully livable," Jarl answered dryly.

"She been a handful?"

"An understatement. She currently has the temperament of a shrew, listens to no one, has no concept of taking care of herself, and has generally been more trouble than any ten women are worth."

Max scratched his chin, chuckling. "She don't take too well to being tied down."

"She doesn't take to being tied down at all." Jarl turned away and reached for the coffeepot on the stove. "Like it strong?"

"The blacker and stronger the better."

"Nothing's changed from what I told you. The doctor said she was to stay completely off the leg for three days. The scar will be a honey, and between the antibiotics and pain pills, she slept most of yesterday. When she isn't sleeping, it would help to have a bulldozer sit on her. Seeing Kip wasn't going to wait."

"Still, sounds to me wisest if I took Kip for a few more days."

Jarl shook his head as he handed Max the mug. "She's through the worst. I can handle both of them, but I'd appreciate it if you'd row out for some clothes from the island and also check on whatever food or things she had left around."

"Sure. Fine place you got here."

The old codger wanted distance from the steady beat in Jarl's eyes. Jarl patiently watched him edge into the other room, apparently captivated by the A-frame cedar cottage.

The back triangular wall was smoked glass and, with the help of solar panels, framed the two-story atrium that was Jarl's hobby. He didn't have potted plants but potted trees: seven-foot-tall ferns, firs, the thick-spined spruce of his native Finland.

Sun speckled through his in-house woods on the main downstairs room that was both a living and eating area. The front triangular wall was also glass, and viewed his clover-shaped cove of the lake. Unvarnished, unfinished cedar made up the support walls. A circular waist-high stone fire-pit dominated the center of the room.

A slash of glass served as a table, and the teal carpet was luxurious and thick, but he'd never bothered much with furnishings. His couch was a relic, the walls bare. He'd created a place of space and simplicity, and being Jarl, every construction detail was perfect. He'd simply balked at furniture shopping.

"A man's place, all right," Max admired. "It's like you're living outside when you're in." Nosily he motioned to the open wrought-iron staircase. "What's up?"

"The loft has a bedroom and bath. And beyond the double set of doors, there's another bath, a shop-utility room, and the spare bedroom where Sara's sleeping."

"All one man needs and more. Sara seen the kitchen?" Max's glance whisked to the slanted alcove leading from the atrium. Cedar cupboards paired with chrome. The two men shared a look of understanding. No man could have too many appliances in a kitchen, and where women put things away, men liked everything out where they could see and get to them.

"Sara has been threatened with a dire future if she leaves the back bedroom, and on the night I brought her home, she barely knew her own name. So yes, she's seen all of it...but not really. Are we done chitchatting about the house?"

Max patted his pockets, searching for a lighter that didn't exist, then repatted on a matches search. "I should go in and see Sara."

"Kip and Sara are just fine alone, or will be—" Jarl checked his watch "—for another twenty minutes. After that Sara's napping. She just doesn't know it yet. And twenty minutes isn't much time, so you'd better talk fast."

"Talk?"

"I've had enough, Max," Jarl said patiently.

Max's pocket-patting grew frantic. "If she'd wanted you to know something—"

"She doesn't want me to know a damn thing. I don't care. Talk. Now."

It took a match and a glass of whiskey for Max to pour out the story. Some of it wasn't news. The source of Sara's fear always had to be her ex-husband, nothing else made sense. Divorce or no divorce, Jarl had guessed she was hiding away from a man she was afraid of.

He hadn't guessed that she'd been involved with a family as powerful as the Chapmans, that she had stolen her son, that she was wanted by the police. And it was impossible for him to believe that there could have been a public scandal over her fitness as a mother.

"You don't know what she went through." Max puffed on his cigar, ranging the length of the living room with his short, squat stride. "She never planned on taking the boy. She went into the custody hearing thinking she'd win. She had all kinds of people to testify on her side, fancy doctors and psychiatrists, all the maids and such that worked at the Chapman house. They all knew Derek Chapman had a screw loose. But the judge said the doctor stuff was biased 'cause they were friends of hers, and the Chapman people turned on her, said she was the one off her rocker. So she lost, but even then she didn't plan on stealing the boy."

Jarl locked his shoulder against a side wall, feeling more or less like someone had kicked him in the stomach. Max stopped puffing on his cigar long enough to gulp a sip of whiskey.

"She spent months fighting the system. She got another attorney, went to Friend of the Court. Hell, she parked at Friend of the Court's doorstep day after day. She got all kinds of sympathy but nobody to do anything. It wasn't her ex-husband that fought her, it was his parents. The Chapmans wanted their grandson, see. It sure wasn't likely they were ever going to have another one, so Kip's their big heir, their future, the whole bit."

Smoke billowed around Max's face in clouds. "What the Chapmans want they get and what did the judge care? Nobody cares about nothing in a divorce trial but money. Kip was just a cog in a big wheel, and maybe it would all have worked out different if they'd taken care of him. I'm not saying they didn't mean to, but the woman's got all these charities and the man's got all that money to manage. One way or another the boy was left a lot with servants—and with his father."

Max kept puffing. "Sara told me a thousand times the bastard was fine some of the time. But not always. Not like you could predict. She wasn't supposed to see Kip, see, but you know her better than that. Nobody could stop her from going to the same church, sometimes catching him in a store. What she saw was killing her. Every time, he looked more sickly, more withdrawn like. He lost weight. She went to the Chapmans. She even went back to see her ex-husband, though I told her not to. I told her and told her..."

Jarl interrupted, his tone quieter than a whisper. "Did he hurt Sara?"

Max stole an uneasy look at Jarl's face. Whatever he saw there propelled the lie. "No."

"So she took the boy."

Max had been about to tell him exactly what shape the boy had been in by then, but a second peek at Jarl's face made him change his mind. Max had no problem with violence—his youth had been a long series of fists and wits survival—but the look on Hendriks' face made him nervous.

He flicked his cigar in the round firepit. "I'm only going to say one more thing. You do anything that would get that boy taken away from her again," Max said quietly, "and you do her a favor and shoot her first."

Sara couldn't remember feeling more like Jell-O. A crisis of problems awaited the first moment she had three ounces of energy. But for now she had no energy. Her leg couldn't conceivably hurt more. Her hair was a mess, she felt as strong as a dishrag, and her bones had the tensile strength of spaghetti.

She was also happy. A little bout with blood poisoning simplified problems. It had reaffirmed for her that being alive, feeling alive, was darned precious, and her company was frosting on the cake. It was also their second visit that day.

Kip had a stool on one side of her bed, Max on the other. A tray acted as a card table. The game was fish. Max played the game as if it were high-stakes poker. So did her son.

"Fours, Max. I know you got 'em." Kip wiggled his fingers, as if to say, "Come on."

"You taken everything I got now."

"Gimme. Gimme, gimme, gimme!" Kip took in two, then reextended his hand. "I know you gotta 'nother one."

Max slapped the third four on Kip's palm with a baleful look. "I'm an old man. I got a bad heart, a cough. But what do you care?"

"You were trying to cheat!"

"Of course I was trying to cheat. We're playing cards, ain't we? And I thought I was the one gonna take you worm-digging tomorrow."

"You still are, Max," Kip said smugly.

"So you think."

Her son giggled so hard that Sara did, too. Exhaustion was stealing over her in waves. She fought it. Everyone that mattered in the world to her was here. Her son. Max. And in the doorway, Jarl stood like a dark-eyed sentry, arms folded over his chest, waiting—and she knew for what.

"Do you have any sevens?" she asked her son.

As expected, the glowering bully in the door moved in as soon as the game was over. "Sara needs her rest."

"I'm not tired!"

"And Kip bargained for a cup of cocoa before bedtime. Max, you want a quick glass of brew?"

He was nice enough to them, but he shook his finger at her after she'd collected kisses and hugs and he'd booted her sidekicks out the door. "You still have a fever. Do not get out of that bed."

She stretched luxuriously, just to let him know what she thought of his implicit threat. She heard his chuckle, and then he was gone.

Eyes closed, her lips curved in a wayward smile that gradually faded, along with her lazy, euphoric mood. Max left within a half hour. She heard the door slam behind him and then the pounce of Kip's footsteps on the stairs to the loft with Jarl.

Her head was fuzzy from the antibiotics and pain killers. Guilt seeped through with no problem at all. Without Jarl, she would probably still be lying in the peach orchard. But instead of freeing him, she'd drawn him in deeper.

She knew from the way he looked at her, the way he bullied her, the way he casually recalled her telling him "I love you'' in the hospital that he was thinking up silly things. Like permanence.

He'd lost his parents when he was too young, that was his trouble. He needed to belong to someone. He needed family. It tore her up every time she thought about him spending Christmas alone.

It tore her up because she loved him. Loved like that first scent of spring after a long winter. Loved like the clutch of a hand when there was nothing else to hold on to. Loved like the beat of a heart, the need to breathe, precious air. Loved with the fierceness of a lioness who'd run in front of a pack of wolves to protect her cub.

But Jarl wasn't her cub. He was a grown man, strong like a rock, sexy as a gypsy... and lonely. She wasn't going to hurt him.

''Where do you think you're going?''

He startled her enough to jump, but she kept peeling down the covers. ''Kip's sleeping?''

''He went out like a power failure. Now where is it you mistakenly thought you were going?''

Attired in one his green T-shirts, she swung her legs over the side of the bed, then had to wait for the pain to stop singing up and down her ankle. Her teeth unclenched in good time, and she framed her words in a nice light tone— the tone she'd been using for two days to protect him. ''Never mind where I'm going. You come near me with one more bowl of soup or one more pill and I'm going to deck you, Hendriks.''

''Now you've got me scared.''

He needed a dozen children. Then he wouldn't be such a domineering rascal. Only she kept picturing his children with her freckles and blue eyes.

Dizzying weakness was no excuse. A woman simply had to think herself strong. ''I am going—'' she eased to her feet ''—to wash my hair. A herd of trampling elephants couldn't stop me, so do yourself a favor and get out of my way.''

''You can't get your leg wet.''

''I don't care.''

"You need to keep the ankle raised. You can hardly do that standing at a sink."

"I don't care."

"Your hair looks fine."

"My hair looks like a reject from a witch's wig factory. Enough is enough of this hypochondriac nonsense. I plan to rejoin life tomorrow, and I know you don't understand this, but I simply can't do that with dirty hair."

"Vanity?"

He sounded charmed at the character flaw. "We're talking basics," she corrected him. "Food. Shelter. Water. Strawberry shampoo."

"Ah." He stroked his chin. "It occurs to me, regularly, how much easier you would be to deal with if you were a man, *nainen*. And that option being out of the question, I guess we are washing your hair."

"Not we—" she began.

"Yes. We."

He scooped her up in his arms and strode to the bathroom, where he collected two towels and shampoo, down the hall, where he continued to discuss the frailties of the female mentality, and into the kitchen, where she looked around with interest once he'd lain her on the counter and turned on the faucets. Studying his room made more sense than acknowledging how hard her heart was thumping from his caveman carry.

"Where's your sauna?"

"Outside, by the lake."

"I love your trees, the firepit. You allergic to chairs, though?"

He said firmly, "You have never been a man walking into a furniture store. They see you coming. They all know what you need, and it all has flowers on it."

"You could take a doberman to guard you next time, and just tell them you need teal and gold. Two couches, Jarl. An oil with water—greens and blues. And—" She stopped, because his grin was out of control. He liked her planning his room. "Or whatever you want," she said briskly.

"What I want for now is for you to lie down."

Her foot nudged a canister of coffee, but there was ample space for her to lie flat on the counter. He bunched a towel under her neck, and she closed her eyes when the first cup of warm water streamed into her ears, down her neck. A little even made it to her hair.

He didn't have an ounce of hairdressing skills. Water splashed everywhere. He used enough shampoo for Rapunzel. His fingers stroked instead of scrubbed, and his face, just above hers, was upside down. He'd stopped smiling and his lips were locked in a grave—very grave—line.

"I've never done this before," he mentioned.

The level of frustration in his voice was near frantic—this, from a man who faced shotguns without a blink. "No kidding?"

"I don't want to get soap in your eyes."

"You won't."

"I don't want to rub too hard."

"You're not."

The trace fever coating her body with weakness had a similar effect on her heart. It touched her, that this hairwashing business had diverted him from the trouble he'd been trying to hide from her. She knew him too well. Neither the teasings nor the scoldings fooled her. All afternoon he'd had something serious on his mind. It probably had to do with her, since she'd caused him forty-eight hours of ceaseless trouble.

She needed to get well and get out of his life. She needed to stop wanting him.

She needed to not hurt him.

Finally he propelled her into a sitting position, and sighed like a war-weary vet because the project was finally done. "Now do we have any other horrible feminine priorities before you get taken back to bed, *kissa*?"

"I would tell you I'd like to shave my legs, but I won't. You have a tendency to get touchy on that subject."

He dropped a towel on her head. "With reason."

But it hurt and offended her when he tried to treat her like fluff. "Jarl, I keep telling you it wasn't like that. It wasn't careless stupidity. Anyone who's physically active gets little cuts and scrapes. That's all I thought this was, and I was hardly going to baby an inch-long scratch."

"It was more than an inch-long scratch two afternoons ago." He pummeled her scalp through the towel.

"But that happened fast. Maybe I was half aware it wasn't healing like it should, but the swelling and infection and fever happened all at once, all at the same time. Even the doctor said—"

"I know what the doctor said. Now hear what I say. You will never use a straight blade on your legs again as long as you live. We'll buy you one of those electric razors for women. Pink or something."

"The generator's chancy enough without wasting energy on something like electric razors."

"Then we'll get you a new generator to go with the razor."

He was so illogical! He whipped the towel off her head and her hands flew to her hair. She knew it was standing up like electric spikes. Rapidly she pushed and patted and mashed. Then it was Jarl's turn to smile. "You look beautiful."

"Good heavens. When's the last time you had your vision checked?"

For that, he kissed her seven times on the way back to the bedroom. Each peck on the cheek was more scolding than sexy, more affectionate than intimate. Intimate was when he patiently stood by the bathroom door, and just as patiently snatched her up again when she came out. "You think it would kill me to walk ten steps to the bed?"

"Your leg's hurting you."

That was intimate, too, she thought. He knew exactly how bad she was hurting. Better sense had to wait. Her leg was now raw. The stupid, lingering fever clawed at her temples. Her brief burst of energy was now floating downstream.

Before she could protest, he'd pulled off his green T-shirt and threaded her arms into a gray one—his again, just as big, just as sexless. There was nothing in his eyes to acknowledge interest in his glimpse of bare breasts, white skin, but his hands trembled when he smoothed the covers to her chin.

"You're overdue for a pain pill."

"I don't want one." The pills were dangerous. When combined with Jarl's presence they created a sweet, warm, yearning euphoria. "You're sleeping with Kip?"

"I was just going to check on him," he told her. He switched out the light and left her.

Her cheek was curled in the pillow when she heard him return. Her eyes blinked wide. She heard a rustle of buttons, the metallic slide of a zipper, the whoosh of jeans tossed on a chair. Without a word, he slid next to her under the sheets. He'd slept with her last night, too, but last night she had been out of her head.

Tonight there was nothing wrong with her head. Malfunctioning vocal chords were her chief problem. His arm drew her into the bow of his body. The T-shirt prevented contact between her spine and the mat of chest hair, but his T-shirt was only so long. Her bare bottom tucked into the curve of his bent thighs. His palm slid under the T-shirt to rest, like coming-home rest, just beneath the vulnerable swell of her breast.

Every movement he made was slow, easy, natural. He didn't shout "you're mine". She simply felt the possessive vibrations. She felt the shimmer of awareness of a man who wanted her. She felt the richness and power of being loved.

There was no chance of her moving. No chance. No choice. Right or wrong, she simply didn't have the will to fight this, or him, tonight.

Just before sleep took her, she felt his warm breath on her cheek. His lips barely touched her ear.

"I know, Sara."

In the silence her heart went on a vacation from breathing.

"We'll deal with it, but not until you're well again. There is absolutely nothing you have to think about now but getting better. And sleeping well. And knowing that nothing and no one is going to hurt you again. Nothing. No one. Believe it.''

Nine

The next day he practiced subtle forms of guerrilla warfare. She wanted a confrontation. He wanted her to take naps. She wanted to know how, when, why and what Max had told him. He was around to ask, but he never entered the bedroom without his three-foot sidekick.

After lunch, Kip climbed in bed with her. Jarl stashed six pillows behind them, and her son, well coached, played Finnish language teacher. "*Yksi, kaksi, kolme.* That's *one, two, three,* Mom. Now you say it."

She said it, one arm cuddling her son, but her eyes were peeled on the devil casually reading a sports magazine in the far corner of the room.

"*Herra* means *guy. Tyttö* means *girl.* Now try those."

Obediently, she tried those.

"*Ravinto.* That's *food.*"

"*Ravinto,*" she echoed, and wished she had the strength to go over to that rocker and shake Jarl. Max wouldn't willingly have told him anything. Jarl was so tricky he could probably make a fox talk, but getting him to talk—figuring out what he was thinking—was something else. To her son, she murmured lightly, "Any chance you know what *kissa* means?"

"Sure I do. *Kitten*. Everybody knows that who knows Finnish as good as I do, Mom."

"I didn't realize." He'd been calling her Kitten all this time. "How about *nainen*?"

Kip scrunched up his nose. "Never heard of it. Jarl, what's *nainen* mean?"

"*Nainen* means *my woman*," Jarl drawled lazily from behind the table of contents for *Field and Stream*, which was as far as he'd read in the past half hour. "It's a tough word to translate without a total connotative understanding, however. It implies something along the line of caveman possession, honor, a claiming, the rights to defend and protect, the right to take."

"Good grief." Kip turned his face up to her. "I didn't get all of that. Stick with easier words, Mom."

"I will." Her voice was faint. So was her head. Over the top of the magazine, Jarl's eyes met hers with the calm, cool satisfaction of a relaxed wolf. Why not? His fawn was already cornered. She said deliberately, "Maybe Jarl could stick with easier words, too. Like basic first names."

"I could," he agreed mildly. "But other men have called you Sara. No other man will call you *nainen*."

Was that a nice thing to say right in front of Kip? He seemed to think he could do and say anything he liked just because she was weak.

And she was weak. Three times a day, bully fashion, he simply turned out the light and closed the door when he decided she needed to nap. She wanted no naps. She wanted to talk to him, and instead she slept half the morning and half the afternoon in spite of herself.

If she wasn't in bed, maybe she'd quit feeling so infernally sleepy. She escaped after dinner—over the protests of two—and made it all the way to the living room couch. Kip fetched three pillows. Jarl tucked a blanket around her and then they ignored her.

The two "men" had a fire to build in the circular stone firepit. Darkness fell as her son knelt on the hearth ledge and built a tepee of kindling twigs, and under Jarl's supervision, lit the match.

Outside, the lake was a black silk mirror, and from his peaked walls of glass, she could see half the stars in the galaxy. Inside, though, were the real stars. Her son's eyes were full of them and his face, raised to Jarl's, glowed with pride. He was so happy.

And he was sleepy, although he didn't know it. Jarl never mentioned bedtimes. He simply lifted Kip from his lap when he nodded off and carried him upstairs.

She waited, folded in darkness and silence. The only light in the room was the small, crackling fire. She didn't need light, only strength. All day he'd done everything he could possibly do to undermine her emotional strength. Building the fire with Kip was close to a last straw. She'd nearly cried. Fathers taught their sons about fire. The pride on Jarl's face had nearly eclipsed Kip's when the twigs successfully flamed.

He loved her son.

She never heard his bare feet on the carpeted stairs, but he was there suddenly, standing at the far side of the room. The red-tinged darkness illuminated his stillness, his maleness, the strong angular bones of his face.

All day, she'd planned and practiced and refined what she intended to say when she finally got him alone. Now she had him alone, and felt the thudding awareness that her prepared speeches were worth refrigerator leftovers. She'd never lied to him by choice, but to protect him. Still, if she tried to evade the whole truth with him one more time, she had the terrible feeling she would be physically ill.

She motioned with her forefinger. "Get over here, Mr. Hendriks."

"Where is it you want me?"

"You know where I want you. Within batting distance." She could see he liked the comment. It earned her a wayward grin, but no obedience. He checked on Kip's fire and then leaned back against the rough stone. Orange flames picked up the gleam of his dark hair but left his face in shadow, which didn't suit her at all. "Kip's asleep?"

"He never even woke up when I took his clothes off." Ankles crossed, shoulders loose, his hands rested on the stone ledge. He looked relaxed, postdinner, the-evening-is-mine relaxed. "Are you going to let me adopt him after we get married?"

Her heart click-clacked like a locomotive on a careening turn. Her tongue went thick. "Don't tease, Jarl. If you talked to Max, then you know there is no possibility of our getting married. Now, ever."

"I talked to Max. You're in a lot of trouble."

"I know."

"Not with your Chapmans. With me. As far as them, you're simply stranded in the middle of the Atlantic without a raft. But your not telling me is serious trouble, *kissa*."

She pushed at the bangs on her forehead. Never mind how calm and quiet his tone, his eyes were a potential mine field. "I should have told you," she said honestly.

"Yes."

"And I would have, if the only issues involved were loving you, trusting you."

"Weren't they? What other reason would you have kept so quiet, except that you were afraid I'd run to the law?"

"I won't lie. In the beginning, I was afraid of that." She tugged the blanket closer to her chin, feeling cold and icy from the inside out. For her, all the emotional dynamics in stealing her son were old news: dread, fear, anxiety, helplessness. His gaze seared on her face with such intensity, exposing the familiar feeling of rawness.

She raised her hand in a gesture of helplessness. "I've also known better than that for a long time. You wouldn't tell on us, Jarl. You wouldn't hurt us. And you're right. I should have told you, because I could see what was building between us, and telling you would have stopped that." She lifted her face. "You should have had the chance to get out, sooner than this, long before you could be hurt. You're not going to get yourself involved with two people hiding from the police, risk getting in legal trouble yourself. I won't let that happen."

He eased to his feet. "You're dreaming if you think I can just walk away."

"You're dreaming if you think you have any other choice," she corrected him, and her voice stayed firm even when he stepped toward her. "You try talking noble and I'll cut you off at the pass. You're not in over your head yet and you're not going to be. There's no yellow brick road, no wizard at the end of the trouble I'm in. There's nothing you can do, no reason at all you should feel badly for walking away."

The firelight lit up his face when he took another step. Bulldogs had strong jaws, but hers was no slouch. "If it hadn't been for my leg, I would never have involved you this much more. So that happened, but tomorrow will be the third day; I'll be walking on it tomorrow. And going back to the island with Kip. Max will help me." Her lower lip was trying to tremble. "And you're going to find someone else. Anyone else. I'm not going to listen to any arguments."

Emotions, subdued since the talk with Max, turned his eyes jet-black. She was pinned prey on the couch, and he leaned over her. Even as his lips touched hers, he knew this was wrong. She had the strength of a newborn kitten, she was not in the mood for kisses, and he was angry with her for drawing him into a mess that a hardware store owner from Pontiac, Michigan, had no conceivable solutions for.

He was angry for not guessing eons ago exactly how serious her trouble was and because she took on every battle with the brave, determined fierceness of a lioness. She protected those she loved. Only along the way, she'd damn well forgotten to protect Sara.

He was angry because her leg hurt her, and because she could have died from blood poisoning. He loved her son. He loved her. To hell with the stories of divorces and custody hearings, it angered him that she'd hooked up with a bastard who had hurt her. He was angry she'd stayed married to him as long as she did. He was angry she'd slept with him. He was angry at the thought of any man knowing her but him.

And because he was angry about so many things, the kiss he laid on her mouth was too harsh, too hard. She froze like an icicle . . . and then melted. Heat shimmered, not a tepid-summer-day-heat, but hell's-inferno. Her mouth molded underneath his, seeking, yearning. Her response did nothing for his self-control.

When both their lungs were starved for oxygen, he broke free. Her eyes closed, but he was having none of that. He hooked his fingers under her chin.

Her eyes were softer than the blue of water. Color, for the first time in days, streaked her cheeks. She wasn't breathing well. She never breathed well when he kissed her. Even when their lips barely touched he felt the heat of a forest fire. For him. For her. And foolishly, her mouth was quivering.

"Think, Jarl."

"No."

"You'll find someone else."

"No."

"I won't let this happen. It can only hurt you and me. You have to get out, not get more involved. You have to—"

He knew what he had to do. Sweeping her up, he sealed his mouth on hers. Her blanket got abandoned en route. She was wearing some nightgown Max had brought her from the island that afternoon, something blue and slippery, making it hard to hold her securely. She didn't want to be kissed and that didn't help. He knew what she wanted: to talk, to argue.

He never argued with Sara.

Soft, like the drape of cotton, her arms stole around his neck. Halfway to the bedroom, she brushed kiss on kiss on his face, his chin, his neck. He guessed she was trying to gentle him.

It wasn't going to work. From the moment Max had told him Sara had been accused of being an abusive, unfit mother, he had not been in a gentle mood. The accusation must have killed her. Knowing that was still half killing him.

He found the bed in the darkness, swept the covers to the floor, and because of her leg, laid her carefully on the bare sheets. Then he stood up, tugged off his shirt, battled with his jeans.

She didn't make the mistake of trying to scramble away, but her voice was fierce and low. "This won't help."

"Yes, it will." It took him three seconds to peel the nightgown over her head, and then he came down, down to the silk-cool sheet and soft arms prepared to placate and soothe him. She was worried because he was angry.

He intended to worry her a great deal more before the night was over. He felt the startled shock wave bolt through her. She was not expecting her navel to be washed by a tongue. He let her worry about that; he had enough on his mind.

He guessed she expected a kiss on her mouth. He kissed her ribs, one at a time. She undoubtedly expected to cushion a man frustrated beyond fire. She was ill prepared for a man to lavish attention on the back of her knee, the flat plane of her abdomen, the breastbone shielding her heart.

He ignored the feminine triangle. He ignored breasts. He ignored lips. His tongue found her wrist. His fingers found the beat of pulse in her throat. The inside of her thigh was unbearably sensitive.

Careful of her ankle, he flipped her over. A dimple marked the swell between her hips. He kissed that hollow, then licked an erotic path up her vertebrae. Only a careless lover neglected the spine. Spine linked to brain. In the brain was emotion. Through emotion, a lover reached soul. She had his, now he wanted hers.

Her flesh was moon-white, and when he'd first stripped off the nightgown, shivering cool. She wasn't cool now. Her breath was coming in patches and her hands were restless by the time he gently turned her onto her back again.

He could remember wanting a woman before, just not like this. He was not a man to appreciate being out of control. His body was burning up, not a pleasant state of affairs. The need to take her flowed over him like liquid fire, but other needs were equally powerful. She was not alone. She was never going to be alone again. She'd been running a long time, but now she was home. And coming apart, beautifully, in his arms.

Sara shivered from the soul. Jarl wasn't being nice. He wasn't being fair; he wasn't being kind. He stole her hands, tucked them over her head where she couldn't touch him. Was that nice?

His lips molded over hers, a tease of tastes and textures that swept yearning through her bloodstream. Then he abandoned her mouth. She lifted her head in a fruitless attempt to recapture his kiss again, but he was already nipping at her throat. Was that fair?

So carefully he avoided contact with her ankle. So boldly he rubbed his chest against the tips of her breasts, making sure she had a thorough awareness of how hard he was, how hot he was, how damn beautiful he was. Was that kind?

"This isn't right," she whispered fiercely.

He heard her. He also felt the way her lips locked on his, the way she clung—desperate, impatient, lonely-wild. Love me, her actions said. Stay with me. "Not right?" Shadows ribboned around them; he wrapped her up in his, made one shadow from two. "This is the only thing that is right. How you open for me when I touch you. How your eyes turn dark, the way you tremble. Come apart for me, *nainen*. Come apart...."

The past was pain. The future fear. She wanted Jarl safe and away from all of it, uninvolved, out of her life. He wasn't listening. He wasn't even trying to listen.

His lips skidded from vulnerable hollow to vulnerable hollow. When he finally released her hands, it was because he wanted the freedom of his own. His palms kneaded, stroked, teased. She bucked toward him when his finger invaded the soft feminine flesh between her thighs. Her body wanted him there. Intimate muscles clamped on his finger, wantonly trying to suck him in deeper. Shameless.

"So ready," he praised her in a voice like gravel. "But not ready enough."

"Yes."

"No. This is not simple. I want to be sure you know this is not simple. This is not making love, *nainen*. This is making very sure you know I love you. That you're mine to protect, to keep, to hold. There will be no more secrets."

A wild, most unwilling moan escaped her throat. He threw a pillow on the floor. Her eyes had long adjusted to the darkness. She could see him. She could see his dark face, the slash of hard lines, the texture like cared-for leather. Copper skin sheathed muscle. His skin was slick, slippery where she tried to clutch and knead. He made love with his eyes open. Her eyes kept squeezing closed, then opening with glazed vision.

She turned aggressive, perhaps from despair. Someone had to love this man. For his Lakka, for his sauna, for his kisses in the rain, for a box turtle that had brought her son to life, for his atrocious fondness for fish, for the way he looked with the wind and the sun in his eyes, for his big, callused hands.

No one could love him as much as she did.

Her tongue took his and her hips arched toward him. She rubbed, nuzzled, wooed. Weakness was her enemy, and pain streaked her leg when she tried to move too fast. She still moved, fast and urgently, and she ignored the weakness.

There would only be this one time. Once, to feel him shudder when her fingers spread on his angular hip. Once, to cup him closer and with an abandon that would have shamed her if it had been any other man. Once, to lure and love. Once, to freely offer him everything she was, everything he meant to her.

Loving him blurred the boundaries of right and wrong. In all fairness she should make him leave her, but nothing in life was fair. If she loved him more, she should have had the strength to deny them both the intimate complication of making love. Only she couldn't love him less.

When he swept her beneath him, she arched to make his possession quicker, wrapping her one leg around him as if she could force that imminent taking. But he was forever a disobedient man.

He paused, perhaps because he knew it would drive her mad. She saw the faintest smile on his face in the darkness, and then she saw that smile die. "So dangerous, so sweet, so much passion. And we're only halfway." His whisper was harsh, a rasp. "You think I'll ever give you up? Never, *kissa*. Never. Never..."

He filled her, all at once. She opened for him. There was no choice—no choice, no room, no lake, no night. Just Jarl. Just a need in her soul to love this man and be loved by him. Velvet strokes and darkness, his whispers as the spiraling rush took her, his slick, slick skin and his eyes...there was so much love in his eyes.

For that so precious gift of love she would have given him anything. A lakeful of diamonds. A soul. A galaxy of stars.

She gave him herself, the only gift she could offer. He whispered her name, over and over, calling her to a place of silver lakes and golden light and soaring freedom. She shuddered on that long wave of silver and gold and then exploded on the crest, with him, by him, for him.

"Sleep, *kissa*."

"I can't." Her arms felt leaden and her limbs were still shuddering with weakness after making love with him. Silently her eyes sought his in the darkness. Silently he met her gaze. Nothing was the same. They both knew it.

"You need your rest," he scolded.

He was wrong. She needed him, and once she gave in to sleep, the night would be over. Lying breast to chest, belly to belly, she stroked, looked, memorized. His hair was all rumpled and thick. His skin was still damp.

He was infinitely warm, infinitely valued, infinitely loved. She wanted to laugh from the sheer joy of loving him. She wanted to coat his flesh with kisses. She wanted to drench him with tenderness, dazzle him with renewed passion, shield his heart from every blizzard, every rain, every cold north wind.

At the very least she wanted the right to hold him, but the minutes kept ticking by. Willing the night to last forever refused to make it so.

He captured her wandering hands and tucked the blanket around her throat. "You're going to get us both in trouble," he murmured.

"I don't see how. There's no one here but you and me." She raised her head and tucked a kiss under his chin. It worried her that she might not have kissed him there before.

"You are going to sleep. Your leg is still sore. You're still weak." Beneath the covers, her fingers skimmed over his inner thigh. His breath caught. "And you seem to think you can get away with anything, just because you're beautiful and you're special and you know I love you."

"Hmmm." Her caresses deliberately teased and aroused, not for her own sake, but for his. She didn't want him to think, not yet. She wanted him happy, and it was only minutes of happiness and lightness for him that she could buy.

"Sara." He grabbed her wrists, then drifted a kiss in her hair, on her cheek. "You need to make love a second time like you need to climb mountains. Behave."

"I don't need to make love at all. I'll probably never need to make love again. You are an extremely special lover, Mr. Hendriks. But . . ."

"But what?" He could barely keep the chuckle from his voice.

"But you gave me ideas I didn't have before. Lusty ideas. Greedy ideas. Sinful ideas. Jarl, your chin is like sandpaper."

"At two in the morning it usually is. It doesn't seem to be inhibiting you in the least."

"I like your chin."

"I can tell."

"I like your mouth. In fact, I like your entire body. Elbows, ribs, eyelashes, everything."

"You're biased." Because she wanted to play, he traced a fingertip down her side. She promptly convulsed and he leaned up on an elbow. "You're also even more ticklish than your son told me."

"I am not."

She was, particularly for middle-rib tickles. He initiated a quick game of slap-tickle-kiss, without the slap, short on the tickle, and very long on the kiss. By the time he'd finished playing he was leaning half over her, breathing like a freight train, his body tensing at every pulse point.

"You know what I'm going to do with you, don't you?" he whispered hoarsely.

"I hope so."

Like it was part of their play, he nuzzled his cheek against hers. Like it was part of their play, he murmured, "I will not let you go, Sara."

She simply raised up and kissed him, hard. "I love you," she whispered, and kissed him again. "And you are not going to be part of the mess I'm in."

"You have no choice. I want to marry you. I want to adopt your son. I want you in my bed, in my life. Tomorrow. Today. Every day."

"Jarl, believe me. There is no way."

His hands dove into her hair, held her face still. In the charcoal dimness, her eyes burned with determined brightness. She was small and weak and bare as a baby...and stubborn as only Sara could be. His whisper was no more than a drag of softness. "I want my ring on your finger. I want your son to have my name, and my baby in your womb. You want my children, honey."

Why didn't he just throw a knife at her? Of course she wanted his children. "Jarl, don't," she said swiftly.

His thumb rocked back and forth on her cheek. "We need to get Kip a dog, take him to the circus. I need to take you to a restaurant. Do you realize we haven't done that? And you have to see my store."

"Don't," she repeated. Her heart thudded pain. There could be no circuses for Kip, no restaurants for her. Everything he said reminded her of the isolation of her life-style—the isolation she would never ask him to be part of.

"Say yes, Sara."

"I can't. You know I can't."

"Tell me you don't want those things."

"What I want doesn't matter."

"You think we couldn't make a good marriage?" He shook his head. "I think I'll still want to make love to you when I'm a hundred and ten."

"Stop doing this," she said helplessly.

Tides sneaked to shore even in the hush of night, as immutable as his gentle bass, as ceaseless as his hands slowly moving over her skin. "I need you, love. Too many years ago I lost a family, a homeland, my roots. This country has been good to me, but a real sense of belonging was never there." He said softly, "Loneliness has sharp edges. I met you and knew exactly how lonely I'd been. You're my niche. My fire on a cold winter's night. And I think you know that kind of loneliness."

She closed her eyes. "Yes."

"I expected to marry sometime, but I never expected...the magic. The specialness of two. The missing you the moment you're out of sight. The anxiety, waiting to see you. Finishing an entire meal with you across the table, and not having the least idea what I've eaten. The sizzle when I touch you. The love, Sara."

She whispered, low, "Yes."

"It's not us you doubt, *kissa*," he murmured gently. "It's the other, the trouble you're in. But you already know the solution to that. There is only one answer. You have to have the right to walk down a street, the right to breathe, to talk to people, to simply live. You can't hide forever, you know that. You can't live your whole life hunted, and you can't—and won't—do that to your son. You're not alone now; I'll help you. We'll find a way."

"No!" Suddenly panicked, she pushed away from him, all the blood rushing to her heart, her fingertips ice-cold. Too easily his words created dreams of living with him and loving him for a lifetime. The dreams were potent, luring, wistful, yearning.

The reality was that of a living nightmare. Acid ate through her stomach at even the thought of returning to the legal system. They'd take her son away again. They'd done it before. Jarl fiercely believed in the values of his adopted country—truth, justice and freedom. He would: he was a good man, an honest man.

But he was too good, too honest, too strong to understand hopelessness as she did. She had pictures in her head of her battered and withdrawn little son that she was never going to forget, didn't want to forget, refused to forget.

"Promise me," she said fiercely. "If you love me at all, Jarl, promise me you won't do anything to have my son taken away from me again!"

"*Nainen.*"

"Promise me!"

"Sara—"

"You don't know! I have to protect my son, Jarl. I have to. I can't think of me, I can't think of you. I can't think of us. I can't make another choice. I don't have another choice."

"Sssh. Sssh." Her cry was fierce, irrational, blind. Jarl buried his frustration and simply gathered her up. So quick, her flesh had turned shaking-cold. His mouth found hers.

"Please, Jarl."

"Sssh." He damned himself for upsetting her, for pushing her when she was still half-ill, for arguing with her when he never argued with Sara.

She shuddered. He covered her. Her eyes seared on his, frantic, dread-dark, helpless. He kissed her eyes closed. She tried to talk. He moved his lips down to crush the flow of words. It was foolishness for her to believe she could continue to live in hiding. She had to know that wasn't possible. She was simply ill and scared.

Also very, very loving. Her mouth suddenly moved beneath his, turned rubbing and heated. Her arms clung, her fingers kneaded. Desire blazed through him. He had the control to temper it and he knew she needed rest.

One small discussion wouldn't wait, though. He had to explain that she had nothing to be afraid of. He would protect her. He had to tell her that she loved him enough to trust him. He had to mention that—foolish woman—she really loved him beyond all rhyme and reason.

So he talked, with his hands and his tongue and his body and his eyes. She told him absolutely everything he needed to know the same way.

It took making love to calm her.

It took making love for him to believe, from the heart, from the soul, how much she loved him. Sara was incomparably honest when she was bare and beneath him. She needed to be held and she wanted to be held. By him.

That was all he really needed to know.

Ten

Sara woke up to bright sun and a warm male body snuggled next to her. At first peek that warm male body had diminished by about two and a half feet and about a hundred and fifty pounds. He was also wearing overalls and gravely perusing a scratch-and-sniff book.

"Morning, lovebug."

"Mom!" The instant she held out an arm, Kip threw down his book and surged on top of her. "I've been guarding you," he told her.

"Guarding me?"

"Guarding you from anybody who tried to wake you. Jarl said he'd shoot anybody who woke you. I didn't, did I? But, Mom, you've been sleeping all day!"

"I'm sorry, punkin." She blinked twice when she focused on the alarm clock. Eleven? And she'd slept like the dead. She hugged her son close, inhaling the smell of his hair, his cheeks, his skin. "Whatcha been doing all morning?"

"Working. *Hard.* Jarl and me made breakfast. Then we fished off the dock. Then we watered his trees. Then we washed some clothes. I turned all the dials, Jarl didn't do a thing. Jarl says it's *sisu* to know how to work a washing machine."

"*Sisu?*"

"*Sisu*'s like *macho*, Mom. And if you don't know what that means, it means like a man. You wouldn't understand."

She understood lots. Her son had a wellspring of energy. He smelled good, his grins were free, and he had a long-running monologue that required little input.

"Jarl says if you're better today you can take a sauna with us. If you're taking a sauna with us, we'll probably all wear towels. When it's just Jarl and me, we don't wear towels, but you're a girl and all. Jarl says that gets tricky."

"Does he?"

Her leg was sore, but not unbearably. More distracting was an intimate tenderness on her breasts and between her thighs. Her body showed disturbing signs of being thoroughly well loved. Her mind showed a disturbing tendency to feel light-headed and happy. Since Mr. Hendriks had kept her up half the night, she couldn't imagine why vibrancy and strength kept seeping into her limbs.

"Max is going to take me worm-digging today, did I tell you?"

Her fingers skimmed his cowlick down. It immediately popped back up. "Did you brush your teeth this morning?"

"Of course I brushed my teeth. Can't you tell?" He leaned over and breathed on her.

"I'm sorry I doubted you. So, getting along pretty well with Max, are you?" Truthfully, she knew Kip and Max were getting on fine. She'd seen them together yesterday. She just hadn't made sense of it yet. Before the accident Kip had been afraid of Max. Jarl had broken the ice of Kip's trusting other men, of course, but that didn't totally explain Kip's about-face for her gruff, overbearing friend.

"You would not believe how much candy Max has at his house."

"No?"

"He doesn't clean anything, Mom. It's wonderful. Everything's a mess. You'd die."

"Probably."

"And we had macaroni and cheese for breakfast, lunch, and dinner. You have never, *never*, let me have macaroni and cheese for breakfast, lunch, and dinner."

"I never have," she agreed, but she was beginning to see how Max had wooed her son.

"He cheats at cards."

"I know that."

"Jarl doesn't. Jarl believes in truth and justice and the American way. You know, like Superman. He bought me some comics. He thought I could read, do you believe that?"

She would have answered, but a dark-haired Finn was bearing down on them from the doorway, dressed in tan jeans and a striped tan and gold pullover. The light colors made his skin look a sunburned cinnamon, his shoulders huge, and his eyes impossibly sexy.

He was missing the blue body suit and the cape, but the Superman image clung to her mind. Unquestionably, Jarl had certain extraordinary powers. Last night he'd turned a careful, sane woman into Jell-O. His lethal imagination had taught her about need. His prowess and tenderness had taught her about want. His hands weaved spells, and his mouth—damn his mouth!—could strip a woman of all reason, all sanity, all sense.

One look at him this morning and she still felt a little bit of fear streaking through her veins. The night before, he'd demanded total trust from her, total vulnerability. She'd given him what he wanted because she'd have given him anything. Now, though, what had been impossibly special and precious had unsettling dimensions. I love you too much, Jarl. Maybe I already knew that, but I never planned on letting you know it, too.

It was too late for her to believe in truth and justice and the American way. But she did believe in honor—her's and Jarl's. Jarl's sense of honor stated that he would never betray those he loved. And her own sense of honor held that one never hurts people one loves.

She loved him enough to want, need, and crave the dream of spending her whole life with him.

Enough to protect him from involvement with a woman who could offer him exactly...nothing.

Jarl loomed over her with a wicked, wicked smile, then pounced. He bestowed just a fast kiss, a disgracefully possessive one, and en route to straightening he managed to scoop up her son.

"Hey, I thought we were going to let her sleep."

"I did, Jarl. I was reading quiet as a mouse."

"Well, we're going to be quiet as mice while your mom has a chance to get dressed."

"We can stay here while she gets dressed."

"Remember what I told you about the towels and the boys and the girls? That gets tricky."

"She'll be lonesome if she has to get dressed by herself," Kip objected reasonably.

"Trust me, she won't be. And you can steal one more piece of coffee cake off the counter in the kitchen if you can do it when I'm not looking."

Kip squirmed down from his arms. "Bye."

She considered squirming, too, the instant her son disappeared from sight. Jarl's gaze swept over her sleep-tumbled hair and face and mouth like he was examining diamonds. "Beautiful," he murmured.

The single word was enough to make her feel edgy, achy. Desperately in love. "I have to..." Her throat thickened. "I have to go back to the island today."

"We will."

She shook her head. "Alone, Jarl."

He smiled one of his tricky smiles, the kind that turned her insides to kindling and the gray matter in her head to soup. Three steps and he reached the bed, bent down and peppered kisses on her nose, then her cheek, then her brow. Sun tangled in his hair. He smelled like the sea. His mouth was soft and taut and warm. "I have two weeks left of this vacation of mine, *kissa*. I'm going to spend them with you."

It was difficult to think when his eyes were that close. When his mouth was that close. When he looked at her like she was stark naked...or would be in two seconds flat if he had his way. She tried, "It would be wiser if—"

"It would be wiser if you didn't argue. Two weeks is a very short time. Too short. There's no way I'll settle for less." He added, low, "Don't deny us those two weeks, Sara."

She wanted to. He could see it in her face. And he could see the imaginary wheels turning. In two weeks, he'd no longer be living on the lake, he'd be back at his store, back at his life, busy forgetting her. Two weeks would make a natural break. A natural break might hurt him less.

He knew she was worried about hurting him.

He also knew that two weeks might not be enough time to coax her to see reason, but it would have to be enough.

"Sara?"

"All right," she said slowly. "Yes." Her gaze seared on his face. "As long as you understand...nothing's changed, nothing's different. At the end of that time—"

"I understand," he assured her.

"He's coming! He's coming!"

Sara straightened, lifting the hair from her nape. A hot August breeze blew off the lake. It was too hot to be harvesting the last of her peach crop in the orchard. Peach fuzz was a dreadful mix with humidity. She felt sticky and itchy from her toes to her navel, but anticipation energized her mood when she saw Jarl striding toward them.

He really was brazenly sexy. His cutoffs were disreputable, his Tigers' cap askew. The sun had painted his skin honey-brown over the last two weeks. Only wearing cutoffs, most of his skin was stark naked. So were her emotions, when he snatched up her son, smacked his cheek, then strode over to her and smacked hers.

"I missed you," he said.

"You've only been gone a few hours!"

"I still missed you."

It just slipped out. "Me, too." That probably just slipped out because it would earn her a rich, private smile between lovers, and then of course a scold.

"Gone a few hours to close up the cottage, and what do I find you doing? Kip, I thought I told you not to let your mom get into any heavy work."

"We weren't working, Jarl. We were picking peaches."

"I can see that. Where are we going with all these bushels?"

They took them to the docks, where Max was picking up the peaches in the morning. Jarl did the hauling while Sara picked the last of her crop. In an hour they were done, in time for a swim before dinner.

The ice water cooled her overheated flesh, but not her mood of anticipation. As they ambled toward the cottage, she tucked an arm around Jarl's waist. "I have a surprise for you after dinner. And until after dinner, you can't go near the living room."

"What is it?"

"Nope, no hints for you."

He immediately turned to his sidekick. "Kip—"

"Don't use a child to get answers, you cretin. Where are your principles?"

She chased them both to the house, stashed them in chairs with lemonade in front of them, and started cooking dinner. The menu was *kalakeitto*, a dish with bacon and salmon, *lihapyöryköitä*—plain old meat balls—and *rieska*, a flat bread. The meal totally lacked balance in terms of nutrition, but it was Finnish. Max had searched high and low to find her the ethnic cookbook.

She'd searched high and low for a way to make this last night together bearable. Her heart kept beating bittersweet, mournful rhythms: you'll never be able to let him go. Her mind, though, was fiercely determined to keep this evening happy, light, easy for both of them.

Jarl didn't help. In fact, he wasn't seated for more than two minutes before he popped up and was opening up pots, standing in her way, sipping things with spoons. "You didn't have to do all this."

But she could see her Finnish dinner pleased him. Still, she scolded, "you're going to be sorry I did. Everything's going to be burned if you don't sit down."

"I'll help."

She wished he wouldn't. Jarl was an excellent cook, but he totally destroyed a kitchen. If there was a dish in the cupboard, he used it. He had a way of strewing silverware over every flat surface. The sink overfilled. And he sneaked kisses on her neck and stole sassy feels of her bottom every time he was close enough.

"My God, you're trouble. Couldn't you go feed the homers with Kip?"

"Kip doesn't need my help. You do. Besides you told me I couldn't go in the living room. What is in there?"

"A present."

"What present?"

She held the spoon where it wouldn't get in the way, reached up and kissed him—the only way she had ever found that shut Jarl up. His eyes immediately changed color. Just from black to black, but there was black . . . and there was black. One was a plain, ordinary eye color and the other had glints of midnight and lusty loving and insatiable desire.

"Behave," she ordered him.

"Did I do anything?"

"You were thinking it."

"Tell me exactly what you think I was thinking."

He seemed so innocent, so interested. A peach-colored blush crept up her cheeks. When she waved the spoon at him he just chuckled. "Later, *kissa*, I won't just tell you what I was thinking. I'll show you. In graphic detail."

All through dinner, she kept thinking about last times. Their last swim together, their last sauna together, the last time she would see his face across a dinner table and to-night ... the last time she would make love with him.

She wasn't the only one who was going to miss him. Kip knew—she'd told him over and over—that Jarl was no longer going to be part of their lives as of tomorrow. She knew that her son was too little to understand or believe that. The separation was going to hurt him, but her little one had thrived and healed because of his relationship with Jarl. There was no way she could protect him from the hurt of that loss, but also no way she would have deprived her son of the richness Jarl had brought to his life.

Or hers.

All day her heart had been busy tearing itself into small shreds. She almost wanted tomorrow to already be here. Waiting for the real pain of separation couldn't be any worse than the reality.

For once, at least, Jarl seemed immune to her feelings. He wasn't acting any differently than it if it were just another day together, one of a thousand yet to come.

The instant dinner was over, he looked pointedly at his empty plate. "Can we go in the living room now?"

She had to smile. "My Lord, hasn't anyone ever given you a present before? You're more impatient than Kip on Christmas Eve!"

"Wait till you see it, Jarl—"

"Sssh," Sara admonished her son.

"I can't tell you," Kip told Jarl sadly.

"Your mother is deliberately driving me crazy, and en-joying it."

"Did you hear that, Mom? Jarl said—"

"I heard. And both of you can just sit still until dessert is over."

Dessert wasn't Finnish, but a strictly American recipe for peach pie. She should have made it before—heaven knew they'd been overrun with peaches for the last two weeks—

but the old cookstove had a marginal oven and making a pie was risky.

Jarl dove in with no fear of risk—what a bottomless pit the man was!—but when she glanced up, she saw Kip was silently poking his fork at the pie, not eating.

"Punkin, you love peach pie," she reminded him.

"Yeah." He poked some more. "My dad doesn't. One time he had some peach pie and he threw it against a wall. Splat. It got all over Grandma's fancy silver stuff. I started laughing, but then..." He poked his pie some more. "I don't think I want any pie."

Sara froze. It was the first time Kip had mentioned his father since she'd stolen him from the Chapman house. He'd seemed to have wiped Derek off his emotional map, blanked out every memory he'd ever had of his father. More than once she'd tried to explain to him about mental illness, about how his father loved him but couldn't help the way he was. Kip had refused to hear, blocked anything she'd tried to say. Until now.

"You know my dad?" Kip asked Jarl.

"No," Jarl said easily.

"You know my grandma and grandpa?"

Jarl shook his head.

"They're nice. You gotta be real quiet in their house, and Grandma has stuff everywhere you can't touch. She always smells good, though." Kip looked at Jarl. "You don't know my dad or my grandma and grandpa?" He sounded as if the idea were incredible. "You must know Uncle John and Aunt Susie."

"My brother and sister," Sara explained.

"I miss Uncle John and Aunt Susie. Uncle John has a horse and three dogs and a rabbit. Aunt Susie laughs all the time. You must know them, Jarl."

"I don't, sport. Remember? I never met you until this summer."

"But that was ages. Never mind, next time we go Uncle John's you can go with u—oh." Kip glanced at his mom. "We can't go there anymore. I forgot."

Silverware clattered as she hurriedly stood up and grabbed the plates. This whole day had been like opening doors in a very big house. On the other side of every one was pain. Her son needed family, aunts and uncles, people who loved him. And Kip had those people. He was simply cut off from them because of choices she'd made. She'd had to make those choices, but the way Jarl looked at her aroused a helplessness, an uneasiness, a rage of hopelessness.

Not tonight. Don't do it to me tonight, her eyes pleaded with him. Then she turned, whipped on the faucet and started rinsing plates.

For a man who didn't argue, he'd fought with her plenty over the past two weeks. He was a back-alley fighter. He never fought fair. He never raised his voice. He never got mad. He simply dropped a comment now and then in that low, gravelly voice when she was least expecting it, least prepared, least able to handle it. Like, where are we going to enroll Kip in school next year, love? And like, you have more courage than any ten women I know, *kissa*. You have the courage to face what you have to face. And like, you think I would let anything happen to you? I'll be with you. We'll find answers together. There are always answers.

He always talked good sense. He always changed the subject before she could fight back, and maybe in her head she knew her chosen course was dead-end wrong, a life-style impossible to live for both her and her son.

But Jarl hadn't survived what she'd had to survive. Ice shards of sick, thick panic climbed her nerves every time he brought up the subject. To risk her son again? Never. Never. But this one night, this one last night, that dominant strength of purpose wasn't doing its job of sustaining her.

Jarl brought two glasses to the counter. His hand brushed her shoulder as he moved back. The quick contact comforted even as it disturbed. "You never mentioned you had a brother and sister."

"Sure do. Both younger," she said lightly. "John's a vet—a year younger than I am. And Susie's only twenty-two—such a beauty! She got all the looks in the family..."

He interrupted her, his tone as smooth as whipped butter...but she wasn't fooled. "How is it they didn't help you? Where were they through all the divorce and custody horrors you went through?"

Her gaze flew for the doorway, but Kip was out of sight. Carefully avoiding meeting Jarl's eyes, she returned her attention to the dishes. "Max telephones them every week so they know we're all right."

"Am I supposed to guess from that that they don't even know where you are?"

She wasn't sure who he was mad at—her, or her brother and sister who he'd never met. "Of course they don't know where we are." Matter-of-factly, she lifted the last pan into the sudsy water. "The first place the Chapmans would have looked for us was with my family. I would hardly have drawn them in, put them in a position where they had to lie. They couldn't get in any trouble if they honestly have no idea where we are."

"And they're happy with that arrangement?"

"They're furious with that arrangement," Sara admitted. "But that's the way it has to be, so that's the way it is." Hanging up the towel, she turned to him with her gayest, brightest smile. "Come on, you. I can't wait any longer to give you my present. Kip!"

It wasn't so hard to divert him. She tugged on one arm, Kip tugged on the other. Laughing, they forced him to close his eyes as they led him into the living room. Sara pulled off the sheet draping the easel. "Okay. Now you can look."

His eyes opened on a room suddenly fallen silent. Too silent. Adrift and nervous, Sara glanced at her oil sketch.

It hadn't been so easy, thinking up a personal gift for him. Art was all she knew. Commercial art had been her field before she married, and it was far more financially viable than children's book illustrations. But that field couldn't be pursued from the island and under her circumstances. Either way, bold strokes and a slash of the whimsical were her talent. Not serious art. Not the good stuff.

She'd tried. The background was lake and sky, and she'd captured his face in profile from a distance because small details weren't her best. She knew his nose wasn't exactly right. She thought his mouth was pretty good, and she'd spent hours blending the exact color of his sun-weathered skin in July. He was alone in the oil, looking at something beyond the painting itself. What she'd wanted to do, needed to do, was capture the way he looked at Kip sometimes. The loving. The intense, quiet richness in his eyes, the blend of fierceness and tenderness in his posture. Jarl was a man you could count on through blizzards and deep water, through famine and flood.

She'd wanted to give him something from the heart. And she hadn't expected wild praise or even necessarily a thank-you, but she'd hoped for more than silence.

"Hey, we don't have to take this so seriously," she said hesitantly. "I never pretended to be a portrait painter. This is just a gift. Heck, Jarl, I don't care if you put it in a closet. It's no big deal."

She was still talking when he plucked her close, wrapped his arms around her, and claimed her mouth...now... hard...with such vitality and pressure that her pulse soared and her nerves felt trampled by the rush. Her heartbeat practiced *whoosh* and *zing*. Her lungs suffered immediate oxygen withdrawal, and her knees wanted to buckle.

When he finally lifted his head, she felt softer than a down feather and was shaken up. The look in his eyes was sober, dark, real.

"Boy." Kip propped his hands on his hips, adult-style. "Guess he likes the present, Mom."

She felt all shivery. "Guess he does."

At two in the morning Jarl found himself restlessly staring at the dust motes on the ceiling in her bedroom. He had to move. Before dawn he always moved to the far bedroom near Kip. Sara had never asked him to, but both under

stood the little one shouldn't find his mother in bed with a
man who was not her husband.

Next to him Sara stirred, snuggling her cheek in the hollow of his shoulder while that word *husband* rolled over and
over in his mind. *Husband* wasn't a romantic word, unlike
lover. *Lover* evoked thoughts of the sweet, the delicious, the
illicit, of secrets and passion and anticipation. Husbands
were simply beings who stuck around through colds and flu,
fractious days and taxes and gray hair.

Blind in the dark, he stroked a strand of hair from her
cheek. Every night for the last two weeks, he'd known Sara
as a lover. There could be none better. His lady always made
love like she never expected to make love again, like he was
her first man, her only man, like lovemaking was its own
island—the only island where she really felt secure.

She called him *lover*.

He wanted her to call him *husband*.

"Can't sleep, love?" she murmured.

His lips touched her forehead. Her skin was sleep-warm
and the night was hot. Too hot to spend it cramped on a
single bunk bed in a room more austere than a monk's cell.

In his bed at the cottage, he could have offered her per-
cale, down, space, coolness, and blankets that never
scratched her soft skin. But he'd failed to coax her off the
island since they'd returned.

He'd failed in more than that.

"Am I taking too much room?" she asked groggily. "I
could move over."

"No."

"What's wrong?"

Her lush alto was wrong. The press of her breast against
his chest was wrong. The tickle of her hair on his shoulder,
the tuck of her leg between his, the scent of her skin was
wrong.

Hiding was wrong, but he'd failed to get that through to
Sara. One word on the subject and she threw up a brick
wall, cast those frantic, wounded eyes at him, and let him
feel the ripples of fear and anxiety shiver all through her

body. Sara not only had a blind spot for her son; she was deaf and mute as well.

She must have sensed his melancholy mood because she leaned up on an elbow, sharply awake in the space of seconds. Moonlight coated her skin with silver, and sleepy or not, her eyes showed the same haunted strain they'd had all day.

She looked at his face. Her fingertips reached up to stroke the furrow between his brows. "Don't think," she whispered. "Thinking doesn't do any good, love."

Her lips dropped on his, mobile, warm, arousing. Her palm slid from his chest to his ribs, then down to his thigh until he roughly snared her wrist. She knew what moved him. It would be easy to be taken under again. Especially these last few nights she'd come to him with sweet wildness and the flavor of recklessness and urgency. She took him to deep, dark, silky waters where a man couldn't breathe without the touch of her.

"Sara." She'd gone still when he grabbed her. To apologize, his thumb caressed the pulse on her wrist where his touch had just been rough. "I love you," he whispered. "Enough to not try and argue with you any more. Enough...to care about what you want and need more than what I do. Can you try to believe that?"

Tears welled in her eyes. She closed them fiercely and reached for him. She had the terrible feeling that if she once started crying she'd never stop.

She understood. He was letting her go.

If she loved him any less, she would beg him to stay. For Jarl's sake, she didn't. For Jarl's sake, she simply and totally loved him.

Eleven

Mr. Hendriks? Mr. Perry will see you now."

Jarl tossed down the magazine and stood up. The woman waiting at the far door was dressed in a dark gray suit with a dangle of pearls. He'd spent the last twenty minutes wondering if she ever sweat. Her hairdo was flawless, her voice perfectly modulated. She moved without sound and her crease of a smile never became less, never became more.

He didn't like her, and the feeling was evidently mutual. She gave him a wide berth as he stalked through the open doorway, then closed the door behind him with a precise little snap. Maybe she had something against men who showed up in her elegant brass and pecan office in jeans and a fisherman's sweater.

Jarl had no particular love for brass and pecan, and even less for lawyers. Grit collected in his throat while he took a second to examine the private office. Thick tomes with gold lettering took up one entire wall, stacked so perfectly that they looked unused. The desk was as big as the town of Pontiac. No fingertips or dust marred the long, windowed wall with its view of downtown Detroit. Outside, the first leaves were turning color on this last day of September.

Inside, Jarl's stomach was turning over, and the battered case in his hand was as heavy as lead.

"Mr. Hendriks?"

"Yes." The man, launching himself out of his desk chair, extended a hand. The only other lawyer Jarl knew was the one who'd taken him for two grand in relation to his citizenship papers. At twenty-one, he'd been too naive to know he was being milked for what he could have gotten free.

He was no longer naive, but his distrust of lawyers was ingrained now. He clasped Perry's hand, assessing what he saw.

The attorney had a private tailor. A diamond was holding his tie down, and he had shrewd, cold eyes. Silver nipped his sideburns, his shoes had a shine like a mirror. Jarl saw sophistication, poise, presence, and a confidence that bordered on arrogance. Perry looked cold from the inside out, a man who took money and winning for granted.

Jarl saw what he wanted, expected, and needed to see. His stomach still rolled acid. The lawyer must have noticed the ice-harsh grip of his palm. Perry's smile was a study in professional reassurance.

"So let's relax, sit down, and tell me what I can do for you, Mr. Hendriks." He motioned him to the cushioned leather chair across his desk. "I must confess to some curiosity for your reason for being here. In your initial inquiry, you asked my secretary whether I handled divorce and custody cases. As she must have told you, I don't. My field is criminal law."

"I'm aware of that. I didn't care if you were a divorce lawyer." He wanted to not be here. He wanted to not feel like he was betraying Sara. He wanted the acid to quit clawing at his gut. "I wanted a lawyer with a track record of winning. Every time."

Harold Perry's eyebrows raised in both curiosity and amusement. "I take it you checked my track record?"

"You've lost three cases in twelve years. If I could have found an attorney who'd done better than that, I would be in his office instead of yours."

Perry's fingers drummed on the desk. His smile never wavered but his gaze shrewdly roamed Jarl's face again. "Most people pick out an attorney because of his specific legal expertise."

"You have a hundred books behind you full of 'legal expertise.' So does any other lawyer. The skill and ability to win has nothing to do with books. It has to do with character." Jarl braced his shoulders in the cold leather behind him, finally accepting that the acid wasn't going to disappear, that the throbbing ache of dread in his temples wasn't going to go away. "I know about your character in a courtroom," he said curtly. "What I don't know, or understand, is the full nature of the lawyer-client relationship. I'm talking about confidentiality."

Perry motioned with his hand. "That's easy enough. In legal terms, what passes between me and a client is no one's business but ours. If I'm representing you, I have the legal freedom to use whatever facts or evidence are available to me to protect you within the full power of the law. For that matter, I could be prosecuted if I betrayed your confidence."

"That's nice. Now to hell with the legal. I assume you could cover those tracks if you wanted to, and the ability or right to prosecute you for a breach of confidence won't help me. I have to know what I tell you won't leave this office."

Perry leaned back, silent. Dark eyes charged on dark eyes, Perry's alive with interest now. He said slowly, "I don't think you're going to buy anything I could say about principles and confidence, are you? So look around you. At this office, at me. I've made it. In fact, I make more money than I know what to do with. I do that by winning, not losing. And I do that by keeping my mouth shut. Not necessarily because it's right, not because it's LEGAL—but because to do otherwise would jeopardize my ability to make a living in criminal law. I don't talk, Hendriks. Because there is no advantage, ever, for me to talk. And you've got me intrigued now. What the hell kind of trouble are you in?''

Jarl started to answer and then couldn't. Sara's face kept shimmering in his mind. Her face, her eyes. He remembered the scent of her skin. It was an unforgettable scent, fragile, vulnerable, sweet.

She was so positive he would never do exactly what he was about to do that she'd trusted him with her life.

Nothing he'd done over the last month and a half was irreversible. He could still back out at this moment. Perry struck him as ice-cold, whip quick and emotionless—not a man Jarl could like or would want to know. He didn't have to like the man, had gone into this office knowing he probably wouldn't. Perry's ability to win was what mattered but the first word spoken would be a Hiroshima of betrayal in Sara's eyes.

He'd rather take a bullet. At this exact instant, he would welcome a bullet.

"At what point," Jarl said slowly, "are you legally considered to be representing me?"

Perry's eyes glinted with humor. "Basically, at the point I take the case, which is rather difficult to decide if you won't get around to telling me your problem."

"I can't tell you my problem until I know you're representing me."

"Hell." Perry leaned over the desk and motioned. "Take out your wallet." When Jarl did, Perry plucked a battered five from the wallet and slammed it on the desk. "Money just changed hands. I am now legally representing you. And if you cause me one more ulcer of curiosity, Hendriks, I'll probably drop you as a client so fast it'll make your head spin."

"Just for the record, I know exactly what your fee is. For that matter, I am prepared to pay double—"

"Dammit, to hell with the money. Would you start talking?"

Again he tried, and couldn't. Instead, he leaned down to lift his bulging, battered briefcase to Perry's desk. As briefcases went, his was a far cry from hand-tooled leather. It was simply a place he kept his tax returns from year to year.

No tax returns filled its space now. The mountains of papers inside represented seven weeks of sleepless nights, and the total of everything he had been able to do on his own.

Custody hearings, he'd discovered, were a matter of public record. Copies of Sara's divorce and custody hearings were backed with reams of newspaper clippings from the past year. He had pictures that showed a woman with shoulder length hair and haunting eyes. Captions labeled her an unstable mother, possibly dangerous. There was one photo of Kip as a baby, being held by his father, looking happy and secure and well cared for. Line after line of printed material damned Sara.

Jarl had read all of it a dozen times. If Perry had asked, he could quote whole areas of the custody hearing by rote. Perry didn't ask, and the rage that had dominated this last month for Jarl was for all the questions he couldn't ask.

Until now, he hadn't dared pursue anything that wasn't simply a matter of public record. To do more—to question or probe too deeply—was to risk exposure for Sara. He'd only pushed that limit once.

Past all the reams of damning evidence was a small, lost file. Sara had taken Kip to a psychologist right after she'd applied for the divorce. The man's testimony had been dismissed because of "bias" in the custody hearing, but his write-up of Kip's emotional state was in there.

Perry barely glanced at the last file, but spent more than thirty minutes in total silence perusing the rest. In the very beginning, he glanced up once, said, "The Chapmans, hmmm?" Jarl saw the claw of interest—gut, greed interest—in his eyes and in the way the man tensed with energy as he flipped through the papers. "Ms. Machine" rapped once. Perry barked at her; she vanished.

Finally, Perry stopped shuffling papers, leaned back, and cast a mild, perfectly controlled smile on Jarl. "To put it mildly, Hendriks," he said gently, "this woman's in deep trouble."

* * *

Two days later was Wednesday. Wednesday nights Jarl closed the hardware store at seven. He loved the store most when it was deserted of noise and people. Then it seemed most like just his. He could identify each aisle by smells: paint, grease, metal, bagged dirt. He always walked those aisles one last time before leaving. He recalled Perry's words. *I know the judge. Barren can be bought but no one'll prove that in this life, Hendriks. Have no illusions.*

He checked the security systems, then turned out lights on the way back to his office, although "office" was a fancy label for the six-by-six cubicle where he did the paperwork. There was space for a metal desk, file cabinet and wall safe, nothing more. Mrs. Kilpepper was his assistant manager, and had thrived on the amount of time he'd been away from the store this last month. Rubber bands were stacked neatly in a box. Pens were in plain sight. She'd thrown out his cache of stale candy bars in the back drawer and replaced them with granola. She was really a very annoying woman.

He grabbed his light jacket, turned off the last light. Words still echoed in his mind. *The first thing we have to do is find out exactly what she's charged with. I'd like to tell you we're only dealing with violation of a custody agreement. But if they have proof she has the boy, we could be talking a kidnapping charge.*

The night wind had rain in it. Pontiac shut down like a well-fed sleepy baby most nights by nine. What was there to stay open for? Stopped at a red light, he flicked the turn signal on right. His house was in that direction; ten minutes and he'd be in it. Somehow, though, when the red beacon turned green, his foot slammed flat on the accelerator, aiming straight.

Kidnapping. Kidnapping.

His stomach growled with hunger. In the rearview mirror his eyes looked hollow, cold, bleak. He couldn't remember if he'd had lunch. He couldn't remember the last night he'd slept.

City lights flew past, then the road turned dark on the two-lane highway. North of Pontiac there were a hundred small lakes, all occupied by cottages. In the summer the highway lent itself to Podunk drivers. Forty was a safe speed. His speedometer read sixty-five.

Get your mind-set off right and wrong, Hendriks. Right and wrong has nothing to do with custody and divorce settlements. Money does. The Chapmans have it to burn; she doesn't.

His speedometer crept toward seventy.

Understand who her real enemy is here. It's not her ex-husband, but his parents. They're the ones who put senators in Lansing and keep a pillar-of-the-community image. Anything wrong with their son, it never made it to the papers. It wouldn't. They own the papers. And if they want their grandson, they'll mow down the whole city of Detroit to get him. Your little Sara isn't any more than a dandelion in a big lawn.

Jarl drove past the tourist lake country. The road emptied of other cars and the houses got fewer between. He must have dragged a hand through his hair a dozen times, trying to shake off exhaustion. It didn't help, and it seemed a year before he turned down the long, sloped gravel road that led to his cottage.

Drizzle was falling by then. He ignored his place and headed for the lakeshore. In seconds, he tore off the protective tarp from his boat and climbed in.

His jacket protected him for a time from the mist, but the dampness crawled into his hair, thickened his eyelashes. The lake was packed with raindrops. His oarlocks creaked, an abrasive sound on a night too silent, and he saw no lights on the island. He didn't expect to. It was already past ten.

He was already sick of all of it. He was just a simple man. He put his shoes on in the morning, had a cold once every two years, and shoveled his own driveway in the winter. None of this was for him. Powerful people like the Chapmans didn't impress him. He'd never aspired to that kind of wealth, that kind of power. He valued privacy. Honor. Peace. Integrity. Truth.

And, yes, dammit, justice. The lamb of Finland had perched next to the lion of Russia for years, always balanced on a cliff edge of careful, careful behavior. Only he was no longer a Finn but an American. Things were supposed to be different in this country. Truth was supposed to be bigger than power.

He tugged his boat onshore, scraping its bottom, not caring. Rain slid down his neck as he crashed toward the woods path. He knew the way blind now, which was just as well. The shiny wet black branches allowed little visibility, and he was moving fast. Heart-attack fast.

Kidnapping.

Exhaustion dragged at him, so did inadequacy, guilt, fear and rage. A man who loved a woman did what was right for her. Nothing else made sense. Sara needed a hero. And all she had was a David facing Goliath without a slingshot, without a stone.

Yellow light shone from her kitchen windows. She was awake. He took the veranda steps in a leap and grabbed the door handle at hinge-ripping speed, but once inside he carefully, quietly, closed the door. He didn't want to wake Kip. He didn't know what he wanted, except to see Sara.

The living room was dark. Throwing off his soaked jacket, he pushed at his boots. Almost immediately his blood pressure started to climb down from the ceiling, for absolutely no reason except that he could hear her humming in the kitchen—hopelessly off key. His *nainen* undoubtedly couldn't sing "Happy Birthday" in tune with a full orchestra accompaniment.

Seven weeks of grueling, driven emotions hovered in limbo as he looked in the kitchen doorway. Insurmountable, unbearable pressures were no less real. He was still inches from coming apart at the seams. Only her kitchen... Lord, what a typically-Sara mess.

A giant pot sat on her stove, smothered in a fog of steam. Jars were lined up on the counter like soldiers. Two bushels of ripe tomatos cluttered her kitchen table, and the whole room reeked of heat and tomato skins and stickiness.

Sara, her back to him, was leaning over a cookbook at the table, her fanny in the air. She was barefoot, wearing a white man's shirt, giant oven mitts, and as far as he could tell, nothing else. Her hair looked windstrewn. Her nape had a dewy line of moisture.

"You're crazy," she announced.

In spite of everything he felt a smile forming on his lips. She was talking to the cookbook. Immediately she resumed her humming, but changed tunes to a mangled rendition of the song about a blue-eyed man who liked to do it his way. He had the feeling the directions in the cookbook were about to go hang.

God, he was tired. "Sara?"

Her head whipped around and up. She was so hot that her cheeks were red, and the smudges under her eyes were as huge as his own. When he saw the way she looked at him, he knew that whatever had been dark, impossible, and insurmountable a few hours before was abruptly worth it. She was worth it. She was worth anything.

"You aren't supposed to be here, damn you," she whispered, and hesitated. Maybe for a second and a half. Before flying toward him.

She clutched, so did he, hard and too awkwardly. She smelled of salt and tomatos and heat. He didn't care. Her mouth rocked under his, as fierce and wild as pain. Under his palm her heartbeat told him mournful, truthful stories about seven weeks of loneliness. She raised her head long enough to scold, "You're all wet!" And then to scold again, "And this is a Wednesday, you crazy man!"

He knew, just as he knew he had to open his store in the morning at seven. What mattered more was how much she blindly, freely, desperately wanted him there. Her eyes gave her away, her hands, her lips.

She stepped back all too soon, the new burn on her cheeks reflecting more than kitchen heat. Confusion shimmered in her eyes, as if she suddenly realized how much she'd given away. She pushed a hand at her hair. "You can't be here. I thought you were never coming back. You can't be back. How could you do this to me now? I look like something the cat dragged in."

"You do," he agreed wryly.

"And you look worse. Darnit, you're working too hard, you look so worn out." Her fingers stroked his cheek. Her eyes filled up, she undoubtedly wanted to believe, with anger. "You've got to take care of yourself."

"I do."

"Better care."

She was trying so hard not to cry. He felt his heart tear. "Such a nag and in bare feet yet. How's my boy?"

"He brought me a garter snake today. I asked myself 'is this fair?' We live on an island. Why and how would one of those dreadful things come to an island?"

She got a grin instead of sympathy from him. He loved her nervous chatter. For a long second there was silence, a moment when both could have succumbed to reality. Both intended to. Neither did. Sara, in an incomparably feminine gesture, motioned to her bombshell of a kitchen. "I'm right in the middle of a mess."

"No kidding?"

Her hands flew up in total frustration. "Jarl, I can't just stop. I'm halfway through everything."

He could see that, and the last thing on earth he wanted to do was can tomatos. What he wanted, what he needed, was to hold her. To strip her bare and take her, hard, swiftly, aggressively.

Instead, he peeled tomatos. Chattering six for a dozen, she whirled around with a clamping device for jars, carrying boiling things from place to place, making puddles on the floor. "It says the jars are supposed to pop. Then you know they're sealed. What does it mean, *pop*?"

"Sweetheart, I have no idea."

"This is my whole crop! Kip loves tomatos. I can't screw them up. Carrots are next. I don't mind if I mess up the carrots. Kip doesn't like them, but he's getting them. They're good for him, but he doesn't like them. But these . . . and the cookbook says to use a knife to get out the air bubbles."

"What air bubbles?"

"I don't know what air bubbles. I've never done this before. If you see an air bubble, stab it with the knife."

She was thrilled when she found an air bubble to poke, and she measured salt in each jar with the precision of a scientist. Some salt made it to her cheek. Some more salt made it to the peanut butter sandwich she made him. A lot of salt made it to the floor, but the exact amount made it to each jar.

At two in the morning every jar was finally filled and cooked and sitting on the counter. He'd wiped all the surfaces he could see. Zombie-white from tiredness, she grabbed a mop, but he heard a screech of triumph when her first jar popped. "Lookit, lookit, lookit!"

He leaned over and duly noted the dent in the one jar that evidently indicated it was "sealed." He expressed proper appreciation but she didn't respond. Her glazed eyes were glued to her jars, but he knew darn well she was no longer seeing them. She was so tired that he doubted she knew her own name.

"What if the rest of them don't pop?" she asked mournfully.

"Is that a trick question? All that happens is that I'll buy you fifty thousand jars of tomatos."

"Jarl! This is an entire exercise in self-sufficiency!"

He took his self-sufficient woman into the living room and installed her on his lap on the couch, arms wrapping her up as cleverly as the bow on a package. Three seconds after her cheek tucked into his shoulder, she was gone, not just asleep but comatose.

He listened to the rain fall. He listened to her jars pop, one by one. He listened to the darkness.

Making love to her was clearly out of the question. It disturbed him that he didn't care, that it was simply enough to hold her, be with her, touch her again. Nothing in these long weeks had made half as much sense as the scent of her. Serenity measured 110 pounds. Peace was the tickle of her hair on his cheek, the sound of her sweet, low breathing, her arms tucked around him blindly.

She slept, trusting him.

He didn't sleep at all. When dawn tipped over the horizon, he carried her into the bedroom, wandered into the next room to kiss his honorary son, and then left. He had to go back ... to betraying her.

"It's time to fish or cut bait, Hendriks."

Jarl, silent, stared out the window at a fog-shrouded Detroit. It was the first of November, and the city was already bleak, winter-dull and dusty.

He didn't have to look behind him to know Perry was pacing the office, hands slung in his pockets. Over the last month he'd come to know Perry as well as a brother, although the relationship was more Cain and Abel than amicable. Perry didn't like people he respected. He was more comfortable with clients he could push, maneuver and charm.

He also wanted to get into court with the Chapmans so badly he could taste it. With shrewd eyes riveted on his client, Perry summarized their situation for the third time. "We have enough on Barren to demand a new judge. We have an affidavit and the testimony of the retired doctor who treated Derek Chapman fifteen years ago. We also have his hospital records from the time of that accident."

Jarl already knew what they had. "It's not enough."

Perry had learned—or tried—to ignore Jarl. Talking to himself was more satisfying. "I'll petition for Browning as a judge. We'll get him. The Chapmans aren't going to get away with padding the witness stand with their employees this time. We've got Sara's psychologist's testimony, the little blonde from the nursery school—"

"What about the charges against Sara?"

Perry slid a dry glance at his client. "As I might have
mentioned to you several hundred times, if she'd get her tail
back in the legal system voluntarily...." Jarl was silent.
Perry sighed. "So. We do things the hard way. What's new?
And even that could be worse. If her situation doesn't whip
up sympathy from an honest judge, nothing will. We'll paint
her as terrified, desperate—"

"You don't have to paint her anything. That's what she
was—and is." Finally, Jarl turned to face the attorney. "I
still don't think we have enough."

"Hendriks, you have a regular habit of confusing which
one of us went to law school. Why do you think I'd tell you
we were ready to go to court if we weren't?"

Jarl had heard the same rhetoric all morning. "Tell me
again what we do from here."

"We file a motion for a new custody hearing, petitioning
for a different judge at the same time."

"And then what?"

"Then we press for speed, which should be automatic.
Not just because custody issues take dominance in the
court's schedule, but because we can push the child's critical circumstances. He doesn't need another trauma in his
life after what he's already been through. If I yell loud
enough, I'm almost certain we can get a hearing scheduled
within a week."

Jarl's face had turned gray, his stomach stone. "As long
as you don't take Kip away from Sara for that week."

On a rare occasion Perry forgot himself and let a streak
of compassion sneak into his tone. "Hendriks. We've been
through this a dozen times. With the charges against her, the
court is almost certain to take the child into custody until the
hearing. They won't put him with an ogre, dammit."

"You can't separate them."

"And Sara," Perry tried inexorable cheerfulness, "will
likely be made some kind of ward of the court. Not jail, but
some kind of protective custody, and you can stop looking
at me like that. I can plead extenuating circumstances from

here to eternity, but the fact is, she broke the law. They'll want some assurances she's in no position to steal the boy again.''

"You can't separate them.''

Perry reminded himself never to take on a Finn as a client again. "Then get her to come forward on her own.''

Jarl shook his head. "There's no chance she'll do that.''

"So we deal from the cards we have. She's still too scared, too sure that Derek Chapman is going to hurt the child, to come forward on her own. It'll wash. Our whole case is based on those same aces.'' Perry's fist slammed into his palm. "The Chapmans are going to get washed and hung up to dry. I haven't looked forward to a case this much in ten years. I know damn well it'll make the front page.''

Jarl tuned him out, needing to think it out one last time. The first day he'd walked into the attorney's office, he knew his motivations had been selfish. He wanted Sara in his life. He wanted the freedom to care for her and Kip. He wanted to live with her, laugh with her, love her. None of that was possible unless she faced up to the trouble she was in.

Now he wasn't so blind. Broken trust didn't mend. Once Sara discovered what he'd done she'd never forgive the betrayal. Without doubt or hope he knew she would hate him after this.

There was still no other way to give her and her son a life. She couldn't live hunted and in hiding forever. Kip needed medical and dental care, schooling, friends. Sara needed a life, the right to breathe without being scared out of her mind. The only way she could do that was to reenter the legal system and win.

Only he knew she wouldn't see it that way. How many hundreds of times had he tried to talk to her? Emotionally, physically and mentally, where her son was concerned, Sara simply locked herself on the other side of a steep, high wall. He knew why. She was terrified.

And now so was he. About a hundred years ago the issues were simple. Loving her—really loving her—should mean having the strength and courage to do the right thing for her, regardless of the cost to himself.

Only the whole thing struck him as impossibly ironic. Sara had stolen Kip because she'd seen no other choice. Desperate people do desperate things. Jarl was now playing with her life because he saw no other choice. And desperation now clawed at his soul, because if he took the choice to battle for Sara's future and freedom, he was going to lose her.

"Hendriks?"

He jerked his eyes toward the attorney again.

"It's still your ball game," Perry reminded him. "But if we're going to move, it's time."

He thought of her eyes—a lustrous, silky teal when he made love to her, full of sky-blue dance when she laughed in the sunlight, smoky blue by firelight. He thought of her naked in the sauna. He thought of her hands in oven mitts carrying tomato jars. He thought of the look of her when she'd keeled over in his arms with blood poisoning. He thought of that first night on the porch, her sweet, yielding kiss, the exact instant when she'd totally destroyed his desire or need for any other woman for all time.

"All right," he said finally.

"I didn't hear you."

"You heard me," Jarl corrected him, and leveled his cold bleak gaze on the attorney's face. "Do it. Make your motion or whatever you do. But, Perry—?"

"Hmmm?" Perry was already striding for the phone.

"Dammit, win." That time Perry might not have heard him, because his voice was no louder than a whisper.

Twelve

―――

Outside, a raw wind blew and snow clouds clustered over-head, but the house smelled like fresh-baked cookies and woodsmoke. It was a good afternoon for cocoa and cud-dling. Sharing his chair, Sara read to Kip from a dog-eared copy of *The Little Engine That Could*.

Kip, his thumb in his mouth, turned the pages at appro-priate intervals. Sara had gently mentioned that he was a little too old to be still sucking his thumb, but then gave up. He rarely did it anymore, and a thumb in the mouth for *The Little Engine* was the same as an institution.

"I think I can," Sara groaned slowly. "I...think...I can." A little faster, and Kip's whole body jerked forward as if he were the little engine striving so hard.

She heard the scrape of boots on the porch, and thought *Max?* "I think I can!"

But it wasn't Max. Her heart soared eagle-high when she saw Jarl's red-and-black jacket through the window on the door. Her heart beat shamelessly, irrationally.

He'd been back twice in the past month, both times in the middle of the night. Both times she knew better, knew it wasn't right, but her stubborn Finn! And her heart was just as foolish, thumping faster than a puppy's tail because he'd sneaked back to her again.

But when he pushed open the door, alarm replaced that bittersweet anticipation. He looked terrible, ill. The lines around his eyes resembled miniature knife blades. His mouth was white. His eyes were sick, empty, as lost as color in a blizzard.

She knew.

Even before she saw the grandmother-plump, soft woman behind him, she knew. Her arms locked around Kip. The book went clattering to the floor.

"So you're Sara." The older lady stepped in with all the poise and gentle manner of a favorite aunt, her tone soothing and reassuring. "And this is Kip?"

Sara's clasp tightened on her son. She rocked him, Kip crushed so close to her heart that he squirmed. She heard him protest. He wanted to get down. He wanted to fly over there and greet the man with those cold, lost eyes.

She couldn't stop looking at Jarl's face. She thought about pain. The ache of pain when she'd lost her parents, the physical pain of childbirth, the emotional shatter of pain from a marriage turned hell. Those kinds of pain didn't compare.

She thought of the moment she had first heard the verdict at the custody hearing. That was pain. The worst pain she had ever imagined, the worst she had ever survived. That didn't compare.

She didn't say, "I never once thought you could do this to me."

She said nothing. She simply looked at him, feeling the soft, secret, vulnerable corner of her heart simply die. All the illusions that sustained a woman's soul about love and trust were gone.

"We have to leave here in twenty minutes, and you're going to eat something before we go."

Sara raised her head at his hard, cold voice and obediently picked up the wedge of toast. Jarl had made enough toast for seven, enough eggs for a platoon.

"It's going to be fine. Browning has the reputation for being a good judge, a fair judge. And you're going in there with bombs, not just bullets, Sara. You want some tea?"

She shook her head.

"I told you about the retired doctor—Zenka—the man who originally treated your ex-husband years ago after his accident. He's prepared to tell the judge what kind of brain injury your ex-husband suffered, and we've got the hospital records as well. The judge can't ignore that kind of evidence. Dammit, eat something!"

Again she tried.

"There wasn't a person who testified against you the first time, with all that idiotic stuff about you being abusive to Kip, who wasn't in the Chapman employ. They won't be able to pull that again."

When she still said nothing, Jarl scraped back his chair and jerked to his feet. His plate was as untouched as her own. Neither had eaten much in the past five days.

At first, it had struck her as humorously ironic that the courts had appointed Jarl as her "protective custodian." The courts weren't too smart. She didn't need to be put in anyone's protective custody. She would never skip town. And leave her son?

She pressed two fingers to her temples, hearing dishes clattering in the sink behind her. The real irony was being locked in his cottage with Jarl for the past five days. She didn't know her jailer.

The man dressed in a navy blue suit had never been her lover. He talked, certainly more than she did, but it wasn't Jarl's lethally gentle baritone. This man talked like a machine delivering messages. The warmth and intensity in his eyes had been replaced by cold belligerence. He never smiled. He never touched her. And especially last night and this morning, his tone had the edge of a barroom brawler begging for a fight.

"Perry got some kind of 'stay,' some fancy thing so that the hearing takes precedence over any civil charges. There won't be any civil charges once you win at the hearing. Sara!"

She had her plate halfway to the counter when she stopped, pale, quiet. Her dark, angry, blustering Finn looked as if he wanted to slam a fist at something.

"Talk to me."

"What is it you want me to say?"

"It's going to turn out all right! Do you think I would let anything happen to you, to Kip?" He took one look at her face and swore, low and hard. "Get your coat."

"I'll finish the dishes."

"Get your coat. We'll be an hour early."

They were more than an hour early. The hearing was scheduled to start at ten. Jarl was pacing the corridors by eight-thirty. The courthouse was old, with elegant wooden arched doorways, tall thin windows and echoing-cold linoleum floors. She'd been there before.

Jarl had found her a Styrofoam cup of bitter-hot coffee and a bench seat. He stalked, back and forth, a hunter with nothing to shoot, a general with no war to fight. Something wrenched inside her each time he passed.

Her silence had never been a woman's game of "silent treatment" but a lack of ability to talk. There was nothing to say. Dread and an empty hopelessness consumed her spirit. Over and over Jarl had explained what was going to be different about this custody hearing, but he missed the point.

She was going to lose her son.

He kept talking about truth and facts and justice and evidence, but she'd had those bullets on her side before. They didn't matter and neither did his fancy attorney, Perry. The Chapmans had money and power—then and now. Nothing had changed that could make any difference.

Waiting clawed at her. The threat of losing her son again distracted every breath she took, slammed into every beat of her heart, shadowed the focus in her eyes. How could she talk?

"Perry's coming. Come on, Sara."

When she stood up, he was suddenly standing beside her. His gaze swept over her from head to toe, taking in her ivory silk blouse, the camel skirt, the strand of pearls. For the first time in days he touched her. He straightened her collar, which didn't need it. He pushed a strand of hair from her cheek, when her hair was already neatly brushed.

Wounded lions should look so fierce, so angry. His fingertips were cold, jerky. His eyes met hers, daring her to deny him the right to touch her. Four people passed, three adult men in expensive suits clustering around a young black man with ice for eyes and a battered lip. "I love you," Jarl said, as if they were the only two people around, his words as haunted as the long, echo-filled hall.

"Jarl..." For the first time in days, she tried to say something to him that mattered. She couldn't.

She knew he loved her. She knew he believed what he'd done was right. She even knew he'd done it for her, but her soul ripped like a rag every time she looked at him.

He'd put her son at risk.

She couldn't forget that, couldn't forgive it.

Perry's greeting broke the eye contact between the two. Like Jarl, he'd chosen to wear a navy suit, but the contrast between men had never been more apparent. The dark suit on Jarl simply leashed a bear. It emphasized his shoulders, his burnished skin, his sea-wild eyes and strong bones. Perry's suit played up elegance and assurance and civilized control.

The attorney took a long look at Jarl, then at Sara. "I can see two of the three of us are going to handle this just fine," he told Sara dryly. "Pity I didn't bring a tranquilizing gun for him. You look fine. Just right."

"Thank you."

He shifted the briefcase from his right hand and took her arm. "You're not overly worried, are you? Everything's going to be fine. Stay calm, stay cool. Look at the judge just like you're looking at me. Getting frantic won't help anything. Believe me, if you've survived living with Hendriks these past five days, this should be a cupcake by comparison."

Perry often talked a lot about nothing. Charming and calming clients came with his territory. She didn't need calming, although five hours later, both Jarl and Perry could have used a leash and a cage. As she could have told them, the Chapmans were experts at surprises.

She hadn't been in the exact same courtroom before, but it had been nearly identical. Pale sunlight innocuously winked through the line of tall windows to the west. The judge sat behind his tall bench with a gavel. Browning was tall, lean and balding, with a cultured voice and weary eyes.

Jarl and Perry flanked her. Before the lunch recess a scattering of people had filled up the benches behind them. Her witnesses. Most of them were gone now. Since she was the one reapplying for custody, her side had had its chance to be heard first.

Through those first hours, Jarl had sat next to her, hunched and tense. Two medical doctors had taken the stand, then Kip's psychologist and his nursery school teacher. Everyone said what was true, and she'd had her own chance on the stand for nearly an hour. In spite of herself she'd had to stop once for the raw clot of tears. Perry had been delighted with her loss of control. Until a half hour ago he'd been as pleased as a smug cat and Jarl was at least breathing.

The Chapmans' side of the courtroom had been empty except for Rolf and Jane Chapman and their two attorneys. Derek never appeared all morning. When their attorney started to talk and still no Chapman witnesses showed up, Sara simply waited with a building, nauseated feeling of dread.

"The court would like to call Rolf Chapman to the stand."

Her ex-father-in-law never glanced at her as he walked past. The look of him, though, inexorably reminded her of what had first drawn her to loving her ex-husband.

Rolf's chestnut hair was streaked with silver. He had a strong, handsome face, a velvet voice, charisma. He talked, you believed him. If you didn't believe him, you wanted to. His charcoal eyes matched his suit, and his eyes reflected integrity, self-assurance, command. God should look so respectable.

He started out by admitting that everything Sara had said was true, which caused Perry's forehead to pleat in a startled frown. The judge to raise a brow, and Jarl next to her to heave back in his chair.

"My son is ill. I don't deny it, or that he's had problems from the time he had an accident as a young man. If my wife and I lied before, it was only to protect our son *and* our grandson."

His voice droned on, and Sara felt barbed wire start to clench in her stomach. She tasted ice on her tongue as she understood the nature of the new game. The Chapmans were no longer fighting for Derek's having custody. They wanted Kip. Alone.

"Whatever has happened before doesn't change the basic facts. No one is in a better position to take care of the boy than my wife and myself. We can offer our grandson every opportunity and advantage: the best schools, the best clothes, a loving environment, stability. Through absolutely no fault of his own, our son isn't physically—medically, if you will—capable of being the father he should be. That woman, though—" Rolf motioned a finger at Sara "—isn't much of a mother herself. My wife and I are only concerned about what's best for the boy."

Perry lurched to his feet with a fancy objection. Sara barely heard him as isolation wrapped her in an emotional fog. She was alone. No one could save her this time. Her heart waited for the attack like a skier waiting for an avalanche; knowing disaster was coming couldn't stop it.

"I ask you to look at what kind of woman she is. She not only stole Kip, but never let us know for weeks whether he was dead or alive. She took him to this place—this island— where there's barely electricity, no amenities, nothing of the environment a child needs to thrive and grow. She was never more than an idealist and a dreamer. She actually believes she can support the boy and provide a decent life for him by selling a little artwork. And the worst, what really pins down her character, is that she formed an irresponsible, immoral liaison with a man. She had a blatant affair right in front of her child."

Again Perry surged to his feet. "Objection. Again, Your Honor."

She blocked him out, she blocked out Rolf Chapman, she blocked out the judge's quiet response. Jarl's face had turned a stunning gray. For five days he'd done everything but set off a bomb to make her look at him, and now he couldn't, wouldn't look at her. His eyes were as tortured as obsidian on fire.

Confusion reigned for a few moments after Rolf Chapman stepped down. Jarl grabbed Perry and muttered something she couldn't hear. Perry spoke to the judge, then the Chapman attorneys approached the bench. Some motions were made, argued. Distracted by Jarl, it took long seconds for her to translate the legalese into English. Both sides were supposed to be finished but somehow weren't. Faster than she could stop it, Jarl was called to the stand.

Shocked and angry, she plucked at Perry's arm when he returned to the table for a note from his briefcase. "What are you doing?" she whispered.

The attorney whipped through his file of notes. "They made a big business out of your affair with him. We have the right to deal with that."

"But not by using him," she whispered fiercely. "Let me go back up there. Let me answer those questions."

Perry laid a hand on her arm, squeezed, and then walked toward his witness. "Mr. and Mrs. Chapman have attempted to prove a lack of moral fiber in Sara Chapman through her relationship with you, Mr. Hendriks. Would you tell this court whether or not you were having an affair with Sara Chapman?"

Jarl's voice had a razorlike edge. "I love Sara Chapman."

"But you were having an affair with her? And openly in front of her four-year-old son?"

"I showed love for her in front of her son. I believe in no different a way than I showed love for Kip in front of Sara. Kip was never aware or around or near anything anyone could have construed as intimacy. Sara made as sure of that as I did."

"But you hardly knew her very long before you started this—" Perry drew out the word "—affair? I'm sure the whole subject raises questions in the judge's mind as to Sara's fitness as a parent, a mother. For that matter it would seem that you're the kind of man who would willingly aid someone who you knew was living outside of the law."

It went on and on. If she had had a bat, she would have swung it at Perry. He was supposed to be their attorney, on their side, yet she watched Jarl grow stiffer, whiter, fumble with terrible care over each question. He was in pain. Didn't Perry see it? Jarl was strong like an oak, not a reed. There was a point where he wouldn't bend, but break. Crack. Shatter.

"Mr. Perry." Her lip bitten raw, she tried to stand. The attorney shot her a furious glance.

"Now, Mr. Hendriks..."

It wasn't that her heart and entire soul weren't on her son, but that she knew Jarl. She'd never wanted to hurt him. She'd never wanted him part of the ugliness. Emotions she knew were dead knifed to life. The one instinct that had dominated her whole life—you protect those you love— consumed her. And Perry...damn him...kept sniping and biting and nipping until Jarl finally exploded.

"You don't understand! None of you do! None of you have the right to talk about Sara like this. You keep talking about her as if she's some kind of criminal, when I doubt she's done a selfish thing in her entire life. You don't know her. Not like I do. And when I first met her she was a woman scared out of her mind, a woman with absolutely no place to go when your system failed her." His fierce gaze pinned the judge. "She never broke your law. She simply obeyed a higher one—the law of a mother to protect and keep her son safe. You failed to do that. All of you, this court, you attorneys, you Chapmans. What choice did you give her? How the hell can you condemn her for taking her son when you're the guilty ones?''

"Mr. Hendriks," The judge said quietly.

"I loved her, yes. You're going to make that into a crime, too? You don't understand. It's impossible not to love her. You don't know how she is with her son. And her character— Look at her character. She was willing to put her life on the line for Kip, give up everything that mattered to her, sacrifice her whole future. Out of love. Good God, what do you want from her?''

The judge was thumping his gavel. The Chapman attorneys were both standing, clipping out objections. Perry, silent, smiled like a fat cat and in due time expressed proper concern for his overwrought witness's tirade.

All Sara saw was Jarl climbing down from the witness stand, walking past her—past everyone—like someone made of wood, unseeing and blind. She covered her eyes with her palm and blinked back the unbearable well of tears. Her whole body shook.

The judge took a fifteen-minute recess, not long enough for her to recover emotional strength that had simply been stretched too long and too far. When Browning returned to the bench, he started with a long, drawling monologue about the interview he'd had with Kip in his private chambers the day before. Following that, he had a speech to give about people who thought themselves to be above the law.

The snap of his wooden hammer was really the first thing she heard clearly. "Unconditional custody is awarded to the mother. The court is willing to consider a motion for visiting rights for the father, not before or until he has undergone a psychological examination determined by a physician of this court's choosing. Grandparents . . .''

To the mother to the mother to the mother. The words kept repeating, but wouldn't register. She didn't believe them. He was going to take it back. If she breathed wrong, he would take it back. So she didn't breathe until Perry tucked a grin at her.

"Hey, what is this? We just won, sweetheart. God, did we win—all the petunias—and as easy as that. Don't I even get a hug?"

Abruptly, blood remembered to flow from vein to artery to heart. "Where's my son?" she said fiercely.

"I believe Mrs. Conroy will have him right outside the door. Why do I have the feeling you're in a hurry to see him?"

She surged past Perry, dodging bodies and briefcases and coats. She wanted her son. Now. But even with that thrumming exultation and relief bursting through her, her eyes unconsciously swept the emptying courtroom.

Jarl had heard the verdict. She knew he had, but the seat where he'd sat was empty. She saw dark heads, but not *his* dark head. She saw navy suits, but not his navy suit. No one, from courtroom to antechamber to hall, remotely resembled a black-haired Finn with brick shoulders and a stubborn mouth.

He was gone.

A sick, sharp ache of unbearable emptiness welled up inside her. She told herself it was irrational. She wanted him gone, didn't she? There was no going back. A successful verdict had no power to heal the real wound between them. He'd betrayed her. He'd chosen to put her at risk, and Kip at risk. The only kind of love that had any depth, any future, any value no longer existed.

For a moment the huge well of emptiness threatened to engulf her; it was that sharp, that real. Then she lifted her chin, determined to think about her son, not Jarl. She couldn't handle thinking about Jarl. Her heels clicked a hollow refrain in the crowded hall, racing now, searching blindly. Finally she spotted the apple-cheeked older woman near the door. The woman had a sidekick, about three foot two, holding a crane in one arm, a bulldozer in the other.

Like a river, the tears started flowing. And then she had him, high in her arms.

* * *

Max heaved himself up and put a heavy hand over his heart. "Sure do appreciate your coming over to help me, Hendriks."

"No problem." Snow swirled in the air around Jarl's cheeks. The day was bitterly cold. He lifted the last board into the room behind Max's garage. There were two dozen in all, none extraordinarily heavy or long. When he cast another curious glance at Max, the old codger's hand flew to his heart again.

"The old ticker just won't let me lift a thing anymore. Can't tell you how much I appreciate your stopping by."

"Like I said, no problem. What are you planning on building?"

"Building?"

"With the boards."

"Yeah, I'm going to build soon." Max pushed off his cap and wiped at the sweat on his brow as if he'd been the one carrying lumber. "Sure handy to have you for a neighbor. No one else around with the summer crowd long gone. Never expected to see the smoke rising regular out of your chimney come December. Didn't realize you'd moved to the cottage permanentlike. Ain't it kind of a long drive for you into your work every day?"

"I don't mind."

"Come in for a cuppa coffee?"

Jarl shook his head and reached down for his jacket on the woodpile. "No, but thanks."

"One cup won't kill you, and I got it all brewed. Got something better to do on a Sunday morning?"

He had nothing to do, but he wanted to do it in private. The call that morning from Max had surprised him, and he hadn't minded helping the old man. Staying any longer, though, wasn't wise. Max was nosy and talkative. He hadn't mentioned Sara or Kip yet, and Jarl didn't want him to. "I've got bookwork waiting for me, but thanks," he repeated. His car was parked on the quay by the bait shop dock.

"Hold up there. Hold up there." Cigar smoke surged ahead of Max as he hustled forward.

Jarl patiently listened to ten minutes of rambling memories about the old days while his earlobes froze and his feet became numb. "That's real interesting, Max. But now—"

"Got another story to tell you. Just one more."

Jarl shifted on his feet and listened to four more. Snow dropped into the lake like disappearing diamonds. Nightfall, a keening wind-blizzard was due. The wind was no baby's breath even now. "Holy Saint Mary," Max said suddenly. "Would you look at that?"

"Look at what?" When Jarl turned his head toward the lake sky, he saw nothing but clustering snow clouds and gray. At first the birds were no bigger than dots, gray-on-gray invisible. They took shape as they soared toward Max's. One dozen, then two.

"Look at 'em. She's let 'em all go. It means she's in trouble." Max rustled three fast steps toward the dock before he stopped, hand on his heart. "I got to get to her. But this old heart of mine's givin' me real pain today. Must be the cold air in my lungs."

"It's the cigars," Jarl said dryly, but for an instant he stood frozen, watching the birds flutter past to land on their cage tops outside the bait shop.

"Maybe I better pop a nitro before I try and row all the way out there. I feel so weak."

"Shut up, Max." Jarl snapped the words like bullets. "Take my word for it, you don't have the acting ability to make it on Broadway. Now what the hell do you think you're up to?"

"Up to?" Max huffed. "Here Sara could be hurt, maybe the tyke. You know what it means when she sends off all the pigeons—"

Jarl's eyes squeezed closed for no longer than a second. "What I know is that Sara doesn't want me anywhere near her. I don't know what you think you're trying to do, but don't. She won't thank you for it. I'm the last person on this earth she wants to see."

Max said peaceably, "Sure ain't my business, you and Sara."

"You've got that right," Jarl said curtly.

"Course I been standing right here next to you. Wasn't me that sent those pigeons, so I don't see how you can accuse me of setting something up when I couldn't have."

Jarl knew that, which was why he directed a fierce scowl toward the island. Smoke fogged out of her clubhouse chimney in the far distance, blending with clouds and snow. She was fine, he told himself. The old codger was up to something. Jarl didn't find it funny, and he wasn't about to be part of it.

"Well, you just stand around being righteous," Max advised him cheerfully. "Probably Sara's on the island with pneumonia. Maybe the lad's got a broken leg. But I'll be the one to row out there to save them." He took three long strides toward the dock, and then bent over with a coughing fit. His face turned red, and from the corner of his eye he could see that Jarl was still standing as immobile as a stone. He coughed harder, hugging his heart.

"Dammit." The Finn started moving, and when the Finn started moving, bulls better not be standing in his way. "Get in the house. Out of the cold."

"But Sara—"

"I'll take care of Sara. I'll take care of you, too, as soon as I get back. Call a doctor."

"I don't need a doctor."

"You will. As far as I can tell, there isn't a thing wrong with your heart, but there will be when I get back and find out you've set up something to hurt her. If you've upset her, I swear I'll clean your clock. Now get in the house. And stay away from those cigars!"

Max looked appropriately offended, but his innocent expression was wasted. Jarl had already hurled up the rope, climbed into Max's favorite bass boat, and taken off.

"I can take you on any time," Max murmured amiably to the wind. "Any time. You think you're so tough, Hendriks? Wait till you see what she's got in store for you."

Jarl forced the boat motor to chopping speed. The icy wind tore at his face. Adrenaline surged to his lungs. In another month, the shallow strip of high land under the lake would be frozen. Sara could be marooned on her island then. Winter was a damn stupid time to live on an island anyway. Her returning had never made sense. She and Kip could have moved anywhere once the custody hearing was over.

Her moving back to the island made as much sense as his winterizing and moving to his cottage. He still didn't know why he'd done it. Didn't know and didn't care, which about summed up the past three weeks of his life.

Nothing was right anymore. Not eating, not sleeping, not his store, not his life. He slept, snacked and walked with guilt. He told himself over and over that he'd done what he'd set out to do. He'd helped her, freed her, seen her through trouble she couldn't handle on her own, but he didn't much feel like a hero. He felt like a bastard.

Because he was. He'd sat in that courtroom hearing Chapman paint Sara the color of a whore because of her affair with him. She could have lost the boy because of loving *him*. He'd had a sudden total vision of everything she'd risked in loving him, and how blithely and blindly he'd interfered in her life.

He didn't want to see her. He knew damn well she didn't want to see him ever again. Max's acting like a fruitcake only poured salt into a gaping wound.

He neared the shore in silence. Waves slip-slopped on the shore, dropped their load of ice-white bubbles, then receded. He moored Max's boat next to hers, and yes, she had a boat now and kept it in plain sight. *She wasn't really in trouble.* The shore brush had long died off. His boots creaked on withered leaves and ice as he tied up the boat and headed inland. *She couldn't be. He'd have known if something was wrong.*

The path was different in winter, a witch's fest of bleak, tangled branches and ice-slick leaves. Wind whipped and burned his cheeks and eyes. She'd better not be out in this weather. He watched her damn island night and day, worried all the time that something could happen to her. *Dammit, she'd better not be hurt.*

Yellow lights gleamed from every window in the old clubhouse, and she'd made a wreath of pinecones for the door. She'd made it, but Kip must have painted it. Red and green splotches cheerfully destroyed the original design. He almost smiled, idiot that he was.

Sara saw his face outside the casement windows of the door. Her heart tumbled like a weed in the wind. He looked cold, red-cheeked cold...and angry...and stubborn... and exactly like Jarl, except that his boots were taking root outside the door. Thirty seconds ticked by. He still hadn't moved.

"Kip!" She whispered. Her son's face popped around the doorway from the kitchen. "Jarl's here."

It wasn't too ethical, sending her son in to do a woman's job, but for a moment she was so afraid. He had a weakness for Kip, had never denied the child anything. Her son galloped to the door like a pony, sprang at the knob, and with cold air blasting in spread his arms as big as the sky. "Hi, Jarl! Guess what! It's me!"

He swooped up her brazen small one, and she only wished she could be that sure of a welcome. In that first instant she saw his eyes close as tightly as his arms closed on her son. A sweet, thick lump formed in her throat.

Someone in the room chattered a mile a minute about Max's horrendous first and only experience in the sauna. Odd that she could hear the silence just as clearly as the beat of her heart. His eyes hadn't stayed closed long. He was looking at her, with starved, hungry, anxious, wary eyes.

"You look healthy." He didn't make it an accusation, but the same as.

"I'm not."

"I don't see any emergency of any kind."

"There is one," she assured him, but the frog in her throat made her tone less than even, less than sure. She'd prepared the speech for days, but now didn't know how to say it. He certainly wasn't moving toward her.

"Your boat's sitting on the shore. You had a problem, all you had to do was row out."

"But the problem was here. Max couldn't solve it, and the pigeons were the only way I had to call you home. Believe me, I was desperate." Kip tugged at her arm, and she nodded swiftly. Her little one tiptoed into the kitchen and grabbed his coat. Unless Jarl was hard of hearing, he should have heard the back door slam. Possibly, hopefully, he would listen to her now when it mattered.

She faced him alone. "I was wrong."

Emotion could get lost in eyes that black and deep. "No."

"I was dead wrong."

"No."

"For God's sake, don't change all your habits and start arguing with me now, Jarl! I know what I'm talking about!" It would help if he'd budge, but he didn't. He hadn't tried to take off his jacket, hadn't even shut the door yet. Wind hurled snowflakes through the opening, and the fire behind her spit and whooshed revolt at the sudden influx of cold air.

She lifted her hands, dropped them again. "It took me some time to understand," she said softly. "Too long, I know. All I could think of was that you'd betrayed me."

"I did."

"All I could think of was that I'd made the mistake of believing in someone—you—when I knew better. I knew better than to believe in anyone. I thought you risked me, risked Kip."

"Sara, I did."

She shook her head fiercely. "There was no way, long-term, I could have survived or given my son any kind of life by hiding. I always knew that, but I threw up a blind wall whenever the future came up because I was afraid. You knew what I was doing."

"*Kissa.*" He slammed the door behind him.

She started breathing again when she heard that slam, and the sound of that rolling two-syllable endearment. "You knew what I was doing," she repeated. "You knew I was locked on an emotional island, that I couldn't get past that fear. Not alone. It took me a while to understand that you made choices out of love, Jarl. It took me even longer to understand how huge and special that kind of love was."

"Sara—"

She shook her head. "Please let me finish. You're a strong man, but you can't always be strong. No one can. And come a time when you're not so strong, I'd like to be there to show you that I love you enough to care about what's right for you. No matter what you think, no matter if it makes you angry or you don't agree. I would like to believe I'd have the courage to do the right thing based on understanding what you need in your life. Not just on what I need in mine." She whispered, "God, I'm sorry, Jarl."

She didn't say anything else. She didn't have the chance. He loomed close, swept her up and crushed her in a jacket dripping with ice and hands shaking with cold. His mouth, pressed on hers, was unbearably cold for all of a second and a half. Then her lips warmed his and her hands warmed his hands, just as she intended to warm his life with hers.

He lifted his head only long enough to scold, "Don't you dare cry."

"I'm not."

"You are. Stop it."

"You believed in me from the first. Maybe not what I did, but in me. How could I have believed less of you?"

"All this silly chatter…" His *kissa*, she was always trying to talk. Always arguing. Always trying to reason with him. Foolish woman, he hadn't known reason from the day he met her. Didn't she know that?

All that mattered was that she was in his arms. Her mouth yielded under his—soft, sweet, delicious. An embarrassing blur of moisture stung his closed eyes, caused by the scent of her skin. He'd been so sure she would never want to see him again.

He took her lips, over and over, in the only communication he could express. His thumb touched her cheek. His fingers combed through her hair. He pressed against her, length to length, vulnerable as only a man can be vulnerable. He came to her raw, less than strong, less than the man who'd been so sure of himself weeks ago.

She kissed him back. She kissed him as if she were the strong one, as strong as a wind blowing free, as strong as a woman who knew exactly what she wanted and needed in her life. She kissed him with the wild abandon of a woman who could protect a man from those moments when he just might be unbearably vulnerable . . . as she had been.

His head reared back suddenly, his breath coming in rasps, his eyes sweeping over her face with powerful, loving intensity. "Where is my son?" he demanded.

"Out." She reached for him again.

"Out where?"

"Out . . . um . . ." Her smile turned to laughter. "He's out pushing your boat, and mine, in the water. Stranding you, I'm afraid. So you'll be stuck here. So you'll have to listen. The homers are gone. You have no way to send for help at all. You're stuck with us for a while. Max'll come and free you in time."

"When is Max planning on coming over here?"

"Spring."

"That's awfully soon."

"Now who's talking too much?" she scolded him, and placed her lips back on his lips where they belonged.

He had a long winter ahead of him. Kip needed brothers and sisters. She needed miniature Finns to raise who didn't listen, who didn't argue, who didn't obey her worth a damn.

In good time she figured they would have to build a house reasonably close to his store. Island living was impractical. Not that she didn't love the place, but, well, everyone needed a refuge, a place to learn and grow and heal when the whole damn world was against you.

She'd found her island in Jarl.

*   *   *   *   *

Silhouette Desire

1989
IS THE YEAR
OF THE MAN!

What makes a romance? A special man, of course, and Silhouette Desire celebrates that fact with *twelve* of them! From Mr. January to Mr. December, every month spotlights the Silhouette Desire hero—our **MAN OF THE MONTH.**

Sexy, macho, charming, irritating…irresistible! Nothing can stop these men from sweeping you away. Created by some of your favorite authors, each man is custom-made for pleasure—*reading* pleasure—so don't miss a single one.

Diana Palmer kicks off the new year, and you can look forward to magnificent men from **Joan Hohl**, **Jennifer Greene** and many, many more. So get out there and find your man!

Silhouette Desire's

MAN OF THE MONTH...

MAND-1

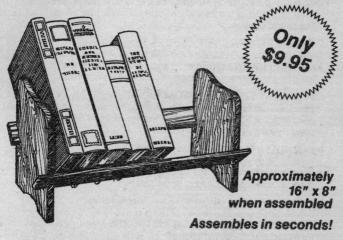

 # Silhouette Desire

COMING
NEXT MONTH

#469 RELUCTANT FATHER—Diana Palmer
Meet our JANUARY MAN-OF-THE-MONTH, Blake Donavan.
Tough. Formidable. He lived alone and liked it that way. His
nemesis was love, but he had one obsession—her name was
Meredith Calhoun.

#470 MONTANA'S TREASURES—Janet Bieber
G.T. Maddox loved his land too much to let Amanda Lukenas
destroy it. He figured he'd offer some old-fashioned hospitality
featuring his own special brand of... friendly persuasion.

#471 THAT FONTAINE WOMAN!—Helen R. Myers
District Attorney Adam Rhodes didn't like Fontaines and Diana was
no exception. She was the kind of woman he knew he could never
control, but one he ached to possess.

#472 HEARTLAND—Sherryl Woods
Friends. Steven Drake and Lara Danvers had once been much more
than that. Now Steven had come back and he wanted Lara *and* her
farm. Could she trust him... this time?

#473 TWILIGHT OVER EDEN—Nicole Monet
Amber Stevenson had to betray the man she loved to protect him
from scandal and disgrace. She still loved Joe Morrow, but the secrets
remained along with her passion.

#474 THIN ICE—Dixie Browning
Maggie Duncan had left a high-powered job and a failed marriage for
her grandfather's cabin. She'd found peace in her solitude—but that
was before Sam Canady arrived!

AVAILABLE NOW:

#463 LADY OF THE ISLAND
Jennifer Greene

#464 A TOUCH OF SPRING
Annette Broadrick

#465 CABIN FEVER
Terry Lawrence

#466 BIG SKY COUNTRY
Jackie Merritt

#467 SOUTHERN COMFORT
Sara Chance

#468 'TIS THE SEASON
Noreen Brownlie